Book #
Roxys
C
S
H

D0935179

Dear Reader,

I loved writing *A Thousand Words* for you. I was reminded of the house where I grew up in Maine—one with a big attic full of dusty old trunks and boxes full of forgotten stuff. I could feel Mary's anticipation as she entered Uncle Lew's attic, because you never know what you'll find! After my dad passed away, it was a bittersweet chore to clean out his attic.

Like Mary, I count my sisters as a blessing. I have three, and though we live far apart, we are close in heart. The time we spend in each other's company is never long enough.

We've never solved a big mystery, but we have our moments. A few months ago, one sister told the rest of us that the new owners of our dad's old house had called her. They had found a ring in the melting spring slush of the driveway. My father had lost that ring a long time ago—it had lain there about six years, undiscovered. My sister went to claim the ring not long after, and it made me think of all the old keepsakes Mary has found that bring to light information about her family and her dear town of Ivy Bay. I hope you enjoy Mary and Betty's foray into an attic!

Susan Page Davis

Secrets of Mary's Bookshop

SECRETS *of* MARY'S
BOOKSHOP

A Thousand Words

Susan Page Davis

Guideposts

New York

Secrets of Mary's Bookshop is a trademark of Guideposts.

Published by Guideposts
16 E. 34th St.
New York, NY 10016
Guideposts.org

Disclaimer: This is a work of fiction. Any references to historical events, real people, or real locales are used fictitiously. Any similarities to real persons, living or dead, is purely coincidental and not intended by the author.

Acknowledgments

Every attempt has been made to credit the sources of copyrighted material used in this book. If any such acknowledgment has been inadvertently omitted or miscredited, receipt of such information would be appreciated.

"From the Guideposts Archives" originally appeared in *Daily Guideposts 2010*. Copyright © 2009 by Guideposts. All rights reserved.

Cover and interior design by Müllerhaus
Cover illustration by Ross Jones, represented by Deborah Wolfe, Ltd.
Typeset by Aptara, Inc.

Printed and bound in the United States of America
10 9 8 7 6 5 4 3 2 1

A Thousand Words

ONE

———◆◆◆———

Mary Fisher loved to travel along Cape Cod roads, taking in the natural beauty of the beaches and marshlands. Her sister, Betty, drove, and from their home in Ivy Bay, they headed down the peninsula all the way to Provincetown, on the tip of the Cape.

Winter highlighted the beauty of Cape Cod in ways the other seasons could not. Leafless trees framed vista after vista of the salt marshes, the snow-dusted dunes of the national seashore, and the empty beaches. Mary sat back and observed the play of morning sunlight on the stone walls and gnarled oaks. In a few months, tourists would swarm the beaches and clog the roads, but right now, the rugged land and the surging ocean belonged to the hardy people who lived here year-round.

"Did the lawyer tell you if we're the only heirs?" Mary asked.

Betty shook her head. "You know as much as I do."

As she drank in the passing panorama, Mary puzzled over their errand. A letter had come to the house yesterday, addressed to both of them. She'd been at the bookshop, and the letter had shocked Betty so badly that she had bundled up against the cold and hurried to the store to share it with her sister.

The wording didn't give many details; it was just a brief and cold statement: "You have been named heirs in the will of the late Lewis Nelson. Your bequest consists of his property in Provincetown, Mass. Please call this office to set up an appointment when you can discuss it with Mr. North." The letter was signed "Robert H. North, Attorney-at-Law." The top of the sheet bore the letterhead for the law firm, which was located in Provincetown.

After some discussion, Betty had made the appointment. Mary had left her assistant, Rebecca, in charge of the bookshop, and they had set off for an adventure on this sparkling January morning.

"I still think it's odd that Uncle Lew left the house to us," Mary said.

Betty glanced over at her. "Me too. Of course, he didn't have any children, but Jean is as closely related as we are. We're all that's left of the family."

Mary considered that. The older generation was gone now. Besides their cousin Jean and her son, only Betty, Mary, and their children and grandchildren made up the extended family. "He always did like us," she said. "He liked Dad too—I think Uncle Lew was closer to Dad than he was to Uncle George."

"Maybe."

"We should call Jean later, after we see the lawyer."

"I think so too," Betty said.

Mary didn't feel she had known Uncle Lew particularly well, mostly because she had lived in Boston most of her married life. Lewis Nelson was actually their grandfather's younger brother. Gramps—Charles Nelson—had been gone a long time now, but Uncle Lew was several years younger and had only passed away a few weeks ago. Mary and Betty had attended his funeral in Provincetown, about an hour away from their home.

They found the offices of Lester & North easily on the main street, upstairs over an antique shop. A sign in the window of the store announced that Attic Treasures was closed for the season. *Too bad*, Mary thought. She loved rummaging through little shops, and she'd glimpsed a bookcase overflowing with old volumes to one side.

The upstairs law office was very much open for business. When Mary and Betty entered, the receptionist looked up from her computer screen and smiled.

"May I help you?"

Betty stepped forward. "Mrs. Emerson and Mrs. Fisher. We have an appointment with Mr. North."

"Have a seat," the receptionist said, removing her reading glasses. "I'll let him know you're here."

The attorneys had kept the original woodwork in the old building, but the furnishings were decidedly modern. Mary sat down on a black leather sofa with Betty. Before long, the receptionist announced Mr. North was ready to see them.

He was tall, with dark hair beginning to show a little gray. He gave a restrained welcome when they stepped into the inner office, and Mary wondered if he was gauging their response to see just how grief-stricken they were over Uncle Lew. They sat down in a pair of well-padded chairs facing his vast desk.

"Well, ladies, you are major beneficiaries in Mr. Nelson's will," he said as he sank into his cushioned swivel chair. "The bequest consists of his residence here in Provincetown, and its contents. His automobile and the residue of his retirement account went to your cousin. She's already received them. It's all in the will, nice and tidy."

So, Jean had not been completely forgotten. Mary was glad.

Mr. North smiled without mirth. "That's the gist of it. Do you have any questions? I assume you know where the house is."

"Yes," Betty said. "We've been there many times."

Mr. North picked up a packet of papers folded into a thick envelope. "The deed and the keys are in here. I'll need for you to sign some paperwork, stating that you've taken possession of the property." He leaned across the desk and handed the envelope to Betty, then opened a manila folder. "I'll just need your signatures on these."

Five minutes later, they had signed the papers and taken their leave of Mr. North and the receptionist and were once more buckling themselves into Betty's car.

"So that's that," Betty said. "Shall we drive over there and see what shape the place is in?"

"We might as well, since we're so close," Mary said. "I'm curious."

It seemed odd that a few scratches of pen on paper had sealed the transaction, and they were now owners of a two-story house with clapboard siding on a lot in a popular resort town.

Betty headed toward the road that held Uncle Lew's house and many other old homes overlooking the water. "What will we do with it?" she asked.

"The house?"

"Yes. We don't need another house."

"We don't," Mary agreed. She'd moved in with Betty after her husband, John, died, and both were happy with the arrangement. They wanted to stay in Ivy Bay—Mary was certain neither of them would even consider moving to Provincetown. Their friends were in Ivy Bay, as was Mary's bookshop. "I guess we could sell it."

Betty sighed. "I suppose so, but that means we'll have to clean it out first."

"Let's talk to Jean before we decide," Mary said. "Someone else in the family may need it more than us. And it could be fun sorting through things. We might find some old family pictures."

"That would be neat," Betty said. "I am curious what we'll find."

A few minutes later, Betty pulled into the driveway and stopped in front of the garage, and they climbed out. Leafless lilac bushes stood knee-deep in snow beside the steps. The white siding looked a bit weathered but not yet in need of painting. The old brick chimney rose toward the gray sky. Mary wished it would issue a puff of smoke, indicating the house was warm and a welcoming fire burned on the hearth, but instead they were faced with the empty—and probably freezing cold—house.

Someone had cleared the driveway and shoveled a path to the front steps. The snow had drifted a little since the job was done, but they were able to walk up to the porch without getting their feet wet. The front door opened into a small hallway, from which three doorways opened—the living room on the right, the dining room on the left, and the kitchen behind it, toward the back of the house. Beyond the living room door, the stairs went up to the second story.

In the entry stood a coat-tree with one of Uncle Lew's wool caps, a furry Cossack hat, and a heavy pea jacket hanging on it. On a small table nearby sat a pewter dish with a book of stamps and a few coins in it. The light-gray wallpaper with fading ivy sprigs had graced these walls at least since Mary's earliest memories. In spite of the cold and the circumstances, she couldn't help a shiver of anticipation. They might find something totally unexpected in this house, and she loved the hint of mystery in that.

She followed Betty slowly into the living room. It looked exactly as it had a couple of years ago, on her last visit to Uncle Lew—sagging plush brown sofa, faux-leather easy chair, beat-up maple coffee table buried in old newspapers and magazines. A worn eight-by-ten braided rug covered the middle of the oak floor. The brick fireplace at the far end of the room had a hearth full of ashes and cinders. To Mary's mind, the one redeeming feature was a full bookcase. If she remembered correctly, Uncle Lew had the entire Time-Life Books series *The Old West* and also some spy novels. Maybe some of those would be suitable for sale at the bookshop.

"No pictures anywhere," Betty said. "Only the calendar and that one motto."

Mary walked over beside her and gazed at the cross-stitched "Home Sweet Home" that hung over the couch.

"Do you think Aunt Maude made that?" Betty asked.

"More likely Great-Grandma Nelson." Mary sighed. "It's a pity there's no art, since they say Aunt Maude was a pretty good artist."

"You'd think he would have kept some of her paintings." Betty set her purse on the couch. "Shall we look at the kitchen?"

"Sure."

The house was chilly but not freezing. Mary heard the furnace come on. She spotted the thermostat on the wall near the hall doorway and went to check it. Someone had left the heat at fifty degrees—warm enough to ensure the pipes wouldn't freeze.

She crossed the hall and peeked into the dining room. The old square table and six matching chairs looked sturdy but not particularly good. Uncle Lew's furnishings seemed to run in the functional line. And no surprises in that room.

They went on to the kitchen, where they found a gas stove, an ancient refrigerator, and a porcelain sink. A quick look in the cupboards disclosed a supply of mismatched dishes and pans.

"I wonder how much of this was here when Aunt Maude died." Mary closed the cupboard door on the glassware and cereal bowls.

Betty's blue eyes grew thoughtful. "I always heard Aunt Maude died young. That's what Gramps told me when I was working on that part of the family tree."

"And not long after they were married." Mary reached deep into the recesses of her memory. "I think Dad told me once that she died the year I was born."

"That sounds about right. I don't remember her though." Betty opened another cupboard. "I do remember coming here to see Uncle Lew when I was pretty small though. If I ever saw her, I've forgotten."

"Maybe we'll find something of hers today," Mary said.

Betty smiled. "Now, that might make all the work ahead of us worthwhile."

"It is going to be a lot of work, isn't it? Packing up everything and getting rid of it." Mary touched an old linen towel that hung on the oven door. The design was so faded from many washings that she couldn't make it out. "Everything in this house looks as if it's been here forever."

Betty chuckled. "Probably all this stuff is what he and Maude got when they set up housekeeping in the forties."

"I guess that's about right," Mary said. "He was ninety-two when he died, or so the obituary said."

"He was ten or fifteen years younger than Gramps." Betty frowned as though doing mental arithmetic.

"I just know Uncle Lew was the youngest of the family," Mary said. "How long do you suppose he and Aunt Maude were married?"

"Maybe five or ten years. I think they got married during World War II. After the war, they settled here. I'm sure she lived in this house at one time."

"Me too," Mary said. "And she's buried in the cemetery where Uncle Lew will be, right?" The cold of New England prevented winter burials, so the graveside service wouldn't be held until spring.

"Right. Remember, the funeral director said Uncle Lew would be laid to rest beside his wife, Maude?" Betty took a deep breath. "No kids. I wonder how she died."

"I don't think Dad ever said."

"Gramps didn't either." Betty opened another cupboard. "Oh, look! I remember this." She lifted out a mug with a hummingbird on the side. "I always loved this. I used to drink my cocoa out of it when we visited Uncle Lew in the winter."

Mary smiled as she gazed at the mug. "I think you should keep that. It will be a nice remembrance of Uncle Lew."

"All right," Betty said, "but you should have something too."

"I'll take a look at his bookcase before we leave." Mary opened the refrigerator and was relieved it was empty except for an open box of baking soda. "Looks like someone cleaned this out after he died. No light—it must be unplugged."

They went back to the living room, where Mary took a cursory look at Uncle Lew's books. A title caught her eye, and she pulled out a biography of Mary Cassatt. She flipped open the cover. "Oh, look! This was Aunt Maude's book."

Betty stepped closer and looked at the signature inside the cover. "Maude Nelson. So she got it after they were married."

"I think I'll take it." Mary laid it on the couch. "I'll go through the rest another time. Let's take a look upstairs."

Betty left the mug with her purse, and they climbed the stairs. Betty's arthritis slowed her steps, but she seemed to be doing fairly well today.

Mary didn't remember being upstairs in the house before. They found two bedrooms, and both had gorgeous views of the shore.

"This is what's going to sell this house," she said, gazing out the window in the room Uncle Lew had obviously used. Provincetown Harbor was laid out below. A few boats moved over the water or rode at anchor, and the cutter docked at the coast-guard station looked like a highly detailed toy. Most of the boats had been dry-docked for the winter, however. Come April or May, the harbor would teem with life.

"It's a prime location," Betty agreed.

Mary got a little misty-eyed as they surveyed Uncle Lew's belongings. His clothes mostly hung in the closet, where the old plaster showed on the walls, or were tucked a bit messily into the dresser drawers. A plastic clothes basket on the closet floor held a few more, next to his scuffed shoes and a pair of lined pac boots.

"Should we do anything with this stuff today?" Betty said.

"I don't know. I'd like to take any papers we find, so we can go through them at home."

"Good idea. If you can find an empty box, you can put everything from his desk in it. And there's a suitcase up there on the closet shelf. While you do the papers, I could pack up his clothes to take to the charity shop."

"All right," Mary said. "Let's wait on the furniture and other things though. We can come back after we decide what to do with the house."

"Sure," Betty said. "We could bring a picnic lunch and make an outing of it."

"That sounds like fun."

They went out into the hall, and Mary saw two doors at the far end.

"Where do those go?"

"The attic, I suppose." Betty walked over and opened the first door, revealing a deep closet filled with boxes and hanging coats. She laughed. "Shows you what I know."

Mary opened the other door. Narrow stairs rose before her into a dim recess above. "Here we go."

"Want to take a look at the attic?" Betty said.

"I don't know—it could be depressing."

"Or enchanting."

Mary chuckled. "All right. But let's pack the things we're taking first. If we get sidetracked in the attic, we might never get back to it."

They worked for half an hour. Mary found a few boxes in the cellarway, and she ended up loading them with the contents of the desk and with books. Betty brought the suitcase and two trash bags of clothing down from upstairs.

"I'm beat," Betty said as they closed the trunk of the car. They'd decided to take so many things Mary had to put some of the clothing in the backseat. "But I still want to take a quick peek in the attic."

Mary smiled. "Me too. Lead the way." They went to the upper hallway again, where she opened the door to the attic steps.

"Come on, let's do it," Betty said with a determined smile.

A shiver of anticipation ran down Mary's spine as she put her foot on the first step.

TWO

—◆◆—

Mary wished she had a flashlight, but the attic windows admitted enough light for her to get to the top of the steps without mishap. She paused and waited for her eyes to adjust. The attic was narrower than the house, and the two walls slanted up to meet overhead. Off to her right, the chimney thrust up from below and disappeared out the slanted ceiling. A window at each end of the long room helped her orient herself. One pointed toward the ocean, the other toward trees and the roofs of other houses.

A porcelain light fixture was mounted in the ceiling, with a single bulb and a pull chain. Mary stepped around a wooden crate and a tall stack of old *Life* magazines tied together with twine. She reached up and pulled the chain. Light flooded the attic, and she realized cartons were stacked two and three deep over much of the floor space, with an occasional piece of furniture stuck among them.

Behind her, Betty gasped. "Look at all this!"

Mary gazed about her at the boxes and bric-a-brac. "If Uncle Lew lived alone for sixty years, how did he accumulate so much junk?"

Betty held up a hand. "Now wait. I'm sure we'll find something wonderful in all of this. Or at least something of great sentimental value."

"I hope so," Mary said. She glanced at her wristwatch. "Let's limit ourselves to half an hour up here, okay? I'd like to get back to the shop this afternoon."

"Fine," Betty said. "How do you want to go about it?"

"Let's just peek into boxes. If we see something interesting, we'll say so. And if we don't find much we want to keep or give away, we can call one of those places that buys all your yard-sale leftovers and hauls them away."

"I guess we could," Betty said hesitantly. "Or someone who would conduct an estate sale here for us and take a percentage of the sales."

"That might be better," Mary said. "We could give the proceeds to a good cause. All right, are you ready?"

Betty looked at her watch. "Ready. Go!"

They moved quickly about the attic, opening boxes and calling out what was in them. A few times, Mary lingered and explored further, but usually she shouted, "Books," or "More dishes," and kept moving.

"Old camera," came Betty's somewhat muffled voice from beyond the chimney. "Venetian blinds."

"Old console radio," Mary said. "That could be worth something." She moved on, in the opposite direction from Betty.

"Clothes," Betty called.

"Phew. Wool blankets with mothballs." Mary coughed and closed the box hastily.

"Hey! Look at this!"

Mary turned. Betty was holding up a blue-and-yellow garment.

"What is that?" Mary walked toward her.

"A sundress. It looks like something that could be worn today, but it can't be new. The other clothes in the trunk are definitely vintage."

"Women's clothes?" Mary asked, moving among the clutter toward Betty. "Do you think they're Aunt Maude's? That would be so neat."

"I can't imagine who else's they would be. And this trunk is full of them." Betty held the tiered sundress out at arm's length. "If she wore this, I think I like her."

"It's cute," Mary said. "I never had the figure to wear anything like that."

"Maybe we'll find some pictures of her," Betty suggested. "Have you seen any photo albums?"

"Not yet." They took each garment out of the trunk and examined it. Betty laid aside the sundress and a challis skirt, and Mary claimed a small vintage purse she thought her granddaughter Daisy might like.

When they'd looked at all the clothing, Mary turned back to where she had left off. A couple of boxes later, she let out a gasp. "Hey, Bets! I found the guest book from her funeral."

"Let me see."

Betty hurried over, wending her way among the boxes.

Mary carefully turned a few pages. "Wow, everyone who went to the funeral must have signed this. Look at all the names." She raised one side of the book so Betty could see. "Here are Uncle George's and Aunt Phyllis's names."

"There are cards under it," Betty said.

Mary lifted the guest book from its flat box and saw that her sister was right. Several colorful cards were tucked under the book. Most had floral bouquets on the front and held expressions of sympathy.

"These are gorgeous," she said. "So quaint."

Betty opened one and peered at the handwritten message. "Oh, wow! This is from Gramps!" She squinted at it and read out loud, "We're so sorry you lost your wife in this tragic way. Ida and I love you, and we're here to support you. Do let us know how we can help."

Mary frowned. "What does that mean?"

Betty read part of the first line again, softly. "Lost your wife in this tragic way."

"What tragic way? I never heard Mom or Dad say anything like that, did you?"

"No," Betty said. "I don't remember ever hearing how Maude died. Just that it was sad she died so young. I guess I always thought it was cancer or something."

"That could qualify as a tragedy." Mary took the card from her. "Well, it's definitely Gramps's handwriting, and it's signed 'Charles and Ida.'"

Betty looked at her watch. "Our half hour is more than gone."

Mary sighed. "We've barely scratched the surface. What do you think?"

"It's been fun, but it'll be noon before we get home. I really didn't plan to spend the whole day in Provincetown."

"Me either." Mary looked around.

A shadowy bundle in the corner under the eaves caught her eye. "Look over there, Bets. What's that?"

Betty peered toward where she pointed. "*Hmm*, something wrapped in cloth. A tarp, maybe?"

"More like old sheets." Mary couldn't help herself. She started making her way past piled cartons, an old chair with the caned seat broken out, and a clothes basket holding a table lamp in pieces.

When she reached the corner, she realized what she had noticed was five thin, rectangular bundles stacked on edge, leaning against one another and the slanted wall.

"I think they're frames." Mary's pulse quickened. "Help me take a look at one."

Betty worked her way in beside her, and they tipped the first one forward. Mary peeled back the layer of dusty fabric wrapped around the object.

She caught her breath as a bright and cheerful painting was revealed. "Look at that! I love it! See all the people? And the shops—Look! The bakery and the grocer…"

"Absolutely delightful," Betty said. "And the colors are so bright."

The sisters didn't move for a moment but stayed crouched and staring at the colorful village scene. People bustled about the streets of the town, going in and out of shops or stopping to gaze into the window of a bakery or art gallery. In the distance was a bit of the shore and the masts of sailboats.

"It's Provincetown," Betty said. "See the monument here?" She pointed to a tall granite tower sticking up above the treetops to one side.

"Definitely." Mary lifted the frame so she could see the bottom of the canvas better. "Look!"

There, in the lower left corner of the scene, was the unmistakable signature of Maude Nelson.

"It's Aunt Maude's!" Mary stared into Betty's delighted face. "We found some of her paintings!"

"Oh my, this is like Christmas," Betty said.

"It's the kind of thing I was hoping we'd find." Mary reached for the next bundle.

"We'd better cover the first one again."

As Betty picked up the sheet they had cast aside, Mary lifted the first painting away from the others.

"Hey! Wait a sec."

"What is it?" Betty asked.

Mary peered down at the back of the frame. "There's a note stuck on the back of this painting. It says 'To Elle.'"

Betty blinked. "Who's Elle?"

"I have no idea." The frame wasn't too heavy, and Mary held the back toward her and studied the little note. The yellowed square was taped to the brown wrapping-paper backing that sealed the framing job. Below the name Elle was a small drawing. Mary thought at first it might be an initial, but it looked more like an inverted *Y* on a straight line. She examined the rest of the paper backing. "There's more tape here, along the edge."

"Where?" Betty leaned closer.

"Right here." Mary nodded toward the discolored tape along one edge of the paper, where it met the wood of the frame. It had once been clear and supple, she was sure, but the old cellophane tape now looked brownish and brittle.

Betty ran a finger along the four-inch strip. "It looks like the paper tore and someone patched it."

"Or," Mary said, "perhaps it was sliced open and then taped up again. See how clean the slit is?" On impulse, she turned the frame up on its side. She was sure she heard something slide inside the backing.

"Do that again," Betty said.

Mary tipped the frame up. As before, she caught the whisper of movement. "I hear it," she said. "And I've got a little pocket-knife in my purse downstairs. Let's find out what's in there."

"I'll wait here."

By the time Mary had dashed down the narrow attic stairs and then down another flight to the living room and back up again, she was puffing. Betty had laid back the wrappings on the other four paintings.

"None of these has a label," she said as Mary wove her way back to the corner. "I checked them all."

"Let me see them," Mary said.

One by one, Betty tipped them forward, so she could view each scene. "I think they're all of Provincetown, but they're different views."

"They're charming," Mary said. "A little Grandma Moses-ish but not so primitive."

"They remind me more of Charles Wysocki's work," Betty mused, looking down at a harbor scene. Another showed the crowded beach on a summer day, and one depicted the downtown during a community picnic or festival, full of bunting and balloons and children. The sisters exclaimed over them but turned their attention back to the mysterious painting that included the Pilgrim Monument.

"Be careful," Betty said as Mary prepared to slice open the paper on the back.

"I will." Mary cut as close to the old tape as she could, but she had to make her incision longer than the original one, so she could get her fingers into the opening. Betty held up the frame and tilted it while Mary explored with her fingertips.

"I feel it. It's paper." She worked it carefully to the slit and a moment later drew out a single, folded white sheet. Betty set the frame down while Mary unfolded it. "Hey!"

"What?" Betty asked.

A spurt of adrenaline made Mary's pulse race. She stared at Betty. "It starts out 'Dear Elle.'"

"Should we read it?" Betty asked uncertainly.

Mary frowned. "Why wouldn't we? I mean, it's old. If Aunt Maude wrote it, she's been dead more than sixty years, and this Elle person is probably gone too."

"I guess you're right. It can't do much harm." Betty smiled. "You read it."

Mary stepped closer to the window and puzzled over the unfamiliar handwriting. The note was penned in blue ink on a sheet of lined paper that reminded her of tablets her mother used to keep for stationery.

> *Dear Elle—there's no time to call you,*
> *and even if there were, I'm not sure I*
> *would. But you may as well know… I'm going.*
> *Tonight.*
> *Lew went too far this time. He hit me—*

Mary broke off her reading and looked at Betty, suddenly feeling she'd overstepped some boundary. Did she really want to intrude into Uncle Lew and Aunt Maude's most private life—especially if the things she learned were painful? Perhaps some harm could come from reading an old letter, after all.

THREE

Betty's lips twitched. "It says that? He *hit* her?"
"Afraid so."

Betty blinked, then nodded. "What else?"

Mary looked down at the sheet in her hand and found her place. "Let's see…"

He hit me, and I don't see any hope for us. The man we've discussed was planning to see me tonight anyway, and I'm going away with him. He is the only person I can trust. I can't tell you where we'll be, but maybe later, after things cool down. Please don't say anything to Lew, but don't worry about me. I'll leave this where I think you'll find it—in the painting I promised you. I will miss you, my friend, despite our recent conflicts. M.

Mary swallowed hard. "Wow."

"That certainly puts a different light on Uncle Lew," Betty said.

"Yes. But let's not be hasty. There could be a lot more to this than we know." Mary stared down at the paper.

"I hope there *is* more to it. It's rather disturbing."

Mary had to agree. Had Uncle Lew really hurt Aunt Maude? "I wonder when this letter was written," she said. "Was it shortly before she died? And did she really leave him?"

"It sounds that way."

"Yes, but…" Mary hesitated. "If she promised Elle this painting, and Elle never got it, maybe she didn't follow through with her plan to leave. Or if she did…We know Aunt Maude died young, and Gramps said it was tragic. Did she die after she left Uncle Lew, or do you think she left and—"

"And lived somewhere else?" Betty asked.

"What I was going to say was, did she leave—or *try* to leave—and die before she could carry out her plan?"

Betty's eyebrows shot up. "Are you saying Uncle Lew might have killed her? Really, Mary! That's too grim. You read too many mysteries."

Mary exhaled in a puff. "You're right. But what happened to her? I think we need to consider all the possibilities."

"Well, Mom and Dad aren't around to ask."

"I wish they were. Or Gramps. We could get it out of him."

Betty shrugged. "We could ask Jean if she knows anything. There's nobody else."

Mary looked at the letter. "There's Elle."

"We don't know who she is."

"I'll bet we can find out." Mary squinted at Maude's signature; it was simply the letter *M*. It was followed by a cryptic sign she didn't recognize. "Hey, where's that note from the back of the frame?"

"Here." Betty held the frame up, back side to them.

"Do you see this doodle on the note?" Mary pointed to the inverted *Y* symbol she'd seen earlier. "Well, look at this." She held out the letter and pointed to the *M* and the small drawing after it.

"What is it?"

"I don't know, but there's one on the note and a different one on the letter." Mary watched for her sister's reaction.

"You think they mean something? You don't think it's just a doodle?"

Mary shook her head. "She seemed to be in a hurry when she wrote the letter, and under stress. I don't think she'd waste time doodling. I think those are something Elle was meant to see—something Elle would understand."

Betty frowned and held the letter up next to the note again. "I suppose it's possible."

"And it's possible we can find Elle," Mary said. She sounded a bit stubborn, even to herself, like a little girl trying to convince her big sister to join her in an escapade.

"Mary," Betty said gently, "you said it yourself earlier: This Elle person is probably gone by now."

Mary sighed. "Well, I think it's worth a try."

"Yes, it is," Betty said. "I'll help you any way I can. But right now, let's wrap these paintings up again. We don't have room in the car to take them with us today."

Mary gazed down at a painting that centered on the town's oldest church. "These are really good, aren't they?"

"I think so. Definitely mid-twentieth century, judging by the hair and clothing styles. There's a car in this one too." Betty pointed to a vintage station wagon in the one that pictured the church.

"Let's shake them all and see if there's anything in them," Mary suggested. One by one, they tipped the frames on their sides and gently wiggled them, but as far as they could tell, none of them except the first made a noise indicating something was inside the backing.

Mary surveyed the treasure trove. "I wish we hadn't put so much in the car."

"I know," Betty said. "I don't think we can fit these in, and it would be an awful job to carry these bulky frames down all those stairs."

"You're right. We'll have to leave them for now. But let me photograph them."

Betty held each painting up near the window while Mary snapped a couple of shots of each one with her smartphone.

"There," Mary said at last. "Now we'll at least be able to look at them and remember what's in them. Let's take the letter with us though. And the funeral guest book and cards."

Betty agreed, and they carefully rewrapped the five paintings and leaned them back against the wall, where they had stayed so many years.

Mary descended the stairs first and then waited to be sure Betty got down safely. She had a lot of work ahead of her, besides disposing of all of Uncle Lew's possessions. Her thoughts played over the new mystery. What happened to Aunt Maude? Mary couldn't help wondering who the mysterious Elle was. What were the cryptic symbols Aunt Maude had drawn on the "To Elle" label and her letter to her friend? And who was the one person Maude had felt she could trust?

———

They gathered up their things and stepped out onto the porch. Betty locked the door and pocketed the key.

"Hello!"

Mary turned toward the voice. A man in the next yard was waving at her. His garage door was up, and inside she could see the unmistakable contours of a snowblower. She smiled at him and stepped down onto the walkway.

"Hello. I'm Lew Nelson's niece, Mary."

"I'm Tom Fuller, his neighbor."

"Glad to meet you," Mary said. "I suspect you may have cleared the driveway for us."

He shrugged. "It didn't take long. I figured someone would show up soon. Do you know what's going to happen to the house?"

"Not yet. My sister and I seem to be the new owners."

His eyebrows shot up, almost meeting the cuff of his green knit cap. "That so? Let me know when you're coming again, and I'll blow the snow out for you."

"Would you?" Mary asked with a truly grateful smile. "We'd appreciate it so much! And we'd be happy to pay you."

"Nah, that's what neighbors are for. Of course, if you start showing the house, you'll need to set up with someone regular."

"Of course," Mary said. "Could we get your phone number? I have a feeling you could help us find someone, if it comes to that."

Tom gladly gave her his phone number. "I wouldn't mind knowing if you decide to put the house on the market too."

"We'll let you know," Mary said. "Did you live next to Uncle Lew for long?"

"We've been here twelve years. Old Lew, he was quite a character."

"What do you mean?" Mary asked. Betty had come down the steps and now joined her.

"Just that he was an old-time New Englander, through and through," Tom said. "Lew wasn't a bad neighbor though. He'd let me borrow a tool if I needed it, and now and then, I'd fix something for him."

Mary nodded. "This is my sister."

"Pleased to meet you," Tom said.

"Would you say Uncle Lew was a good-tempered person?" Betty asked.

Mary was surprised at her question, but Betty must be wondering about the same thing she was: Could Uncle Lew really have gotten angry enough to strike his wife, or worse?

"He had his moments," Tom said, "but overall, I'd say he was an average guy. He'd get angry once in a while—you know, if the car battery went flat or something like that. But he got over it quick."

Mary nodded. "That's good to hear. We used to visit him occasionally, but we're realizing how much we didn't know about him."

Tom smiled. "That happens. Well, it's nice to meet you ladies."

"Same here," Mary said, and Betty murmured, "You too."

Mary opened the back door of the car and stuck her last bundles in between bags of clothing. When she got in the front, Betty had the engine running.

"You know, we're not far from the cemetery," Mary said.

Betty arched her eyebrows. "Do you want to stop by and see if we can find the headstone?"

"If it's plowed, sure. I'd like to see what it says about Aunt Maude."

Betty drove to the cemetery and rolled her car in through the iron gate.

"Dad brought me here once," Mary said. "I think it's over there." She waved toward the crypt. Betty drove as close as she could, and they got out. Not all the paths between the rows of headstones were plowed, but they walked along on packed snow, reading names on the upright stones.

"There it is—Nelson," Betty said after a couple of minutes. "Can you read it from here? My feet are getting cold, and I don't want to try to get closer in these shoes."

Mary squinted at the distant granite stone with *Nelson* engraved on the front in large letters. Below it were the words *Lewis 1920–* and *Maude 1923–*. She looked at Betty. "That's odd. There's no death date for either of them. What do you think that means?"

"I don't know," Betty said. "Maybe he had the birth dates done in advance. You'd think Aunt Maude's death date would have been added at some point though."

Mary frowned. "It says 'Maude 1923 to…' nothing."

They stood gazing across the snow for several seconds.

A puff of vapor rose when Betty exhaled. "Well, I'm hungry. Do you want to get something to eat before we leave town?"

"It's only an hour to home," Mary said.

"Let's get going, then. We've got our painting class tonight, and I should get some rest beforehand."

The warmth of the car's heater welcomed them, and Betty turned toward Ivy Bay. When they reached the house, they ate a quick lunch. Mary encouraged Betty to lie down afterward. She hoped their full morning hadn't worn Betty out. She put her cat, Gus, in his carrier, then hurried to the bookshop.

"Hello," Rebecca called cheerfully as Mary entered. Two customers were browsing the books, one in the children's section and one in the hard-boiled police mysteries.

"Hi." Mary released Gus from the carrier and then took off her hat and gloves and put them under the counter with her purse. "Everything all right here?"

Rebecca nodded. "It was a little slow this morning, so between customers, I packaged the books for that mail order we got yesterday. Oh, and a box came. I think it's those cozy mysteries you ordered."

"Terrific—and you saved it so we could open it together!" Mary smiled as she headed to the back room to hang up her coat. While the winter days could be slow, she found enough traffic came through the store to justify keeping it open.

When she returned to the main part of the store, she saw Henry Woodrow, one of her oldest and dearest friends, talking to Rebecca.

"Hello, Henry," she called.

He turned toward her, smiling. "Rebecca was just telling me that you and Betty have been gallivanting."

Mary laughed. "We sure have." They chatted for a few minutes, and she told him about the house and the paintings in the attic. "It was really quite a find."

"Sounds like it. I wouldn't mind seeing them sometime." A customer entered, and Henry said, "Well, I'll just take a look at what you've gotten in for new books. You ladies have work to do."

"Good to see you, Henry." Mary went to assist the new customer.

She and Rebecca had a pleasant afternoon, and the sales were moderate. The highlight of the afternoon was opening the carton of cozies and arranging them on the front table where Mary liked to display new merchandise.

At five, Mary sent Rebecca home, and an hour later, she locked up and returned to the house. Betty had a light supper ready.

"I'm really looking forward to tonight's class," Mary said as they sat down for broccoli-cheese soup, salad, and sourdough bread.

"So am I. The first two sessions were a lot of fun." Betty smiled and shook her head. "Tea, Paint, and Sympathy. I wonder how Brooke came up with that title."

"It fits what she's offering," Mary said. "I never thought I had much artistic talent, but what I did last time wasn't half bad, if I do say so myself."

"I liked your still life a lot," Betty said. "And I learned a lot from that class."

Mary smiled. "Brooke's a good teacher. I know I have a lot to learn. I can only improve, right?"

"That goes for both of us." Betty sobered as she buttered her bread. "I'd like to get good enough to paint the marsh. I love the way it looks in the morning."

"Tell Brooke. Maybe she can give you some specific pointers."

"I think I'll wait until I learn a little more about technique before I try it," Betty said. "Besides, it's too cold now to sit out in the marsh and try to paint."

When they got to the fellowship hall at Grace Church, four other women and two men were setting out their painting supplies. Brooke had provided some easels, and a few people, including Betty, came with their own. Brooke's mother, Linda Freeman, was setting out the refreshments— the "Tea" part of the meetings—while Brooke went around speaking to each of the students.

Brooke, who was a member of Grace Church and helped organize the schedule for nursery workers, was expecting her own first child soon. When she approached Mary and Betty's area, Mary greeted her warmly.

"Hello, Brooke. How are you feeling?"

Brooke smiled and patted her protruding abdomen. "Not too bad, but I'll be glad when this little one makes her appearance."

"That's an understatement," Brooke's mother said, coming up behind her. "I, for one, can hardly wait to hold that precious little angel!"

Mary glanced at her sister. Betty seemed a bit taken aback by Mrs. Freeman's forwardness.

"I'll bet," Mary said. She smiled at Brooke. "So, you know it's a girl?"

"Yes, we found out a few weeks ago. Bill and I are really excited about it. Bill painted the nursery this week—"

"It's the most gorgeous buttercream color," her mother said. "I helped pick it out."

"Yes," Brooke said with a tight smile. "Well, it's time to get started. Mom, are you going to join the class tonight?"

"No, honey, I think I'll just sit back and watch and have the tea ready whenever you decide to take a break."

"Okay, thanks." Brooke walked to the center of the circle of easels. "Hello, everybody. Tonight, we're going to create a different sort of painting than we did last time. But first, we'll start with a short technique lesson. Even though I want to get everyone painting as quickly as possible, I know how important technique is, and so in each session, we'll focus first on something that should help you make your painting better. Tonight's topic is brushwork."

Mary appreciated Brooke's teaching style. She demonstrated the new material on her own easel, after which she circled the group several times, commenting and helping each individual get comfortable with the new information. Tonight, she showed them all how to load their brushes and apply different thicknesses of paint in order to get a variety of effects. She also showed how using different brushes or a spatula could enhance the painting.

After the lesson, each student practiced the methods on thick watercolor paper, and then they were instructed to start working on a landscape that would include earth, rocks, bushes, and at least one tree. Mary decided to try to paint a sand dune with beach grass and a few shrubs. She put a tree in the foreground, and off in the distance, she would fill in a glimpse of the bay. For a beginner, it felt ambitious, but she wanted to practice all the new techniques Brooke had shown them.

When the instructor reached Betty's easel, she said, "Oh, you're painting the bog!"

"Yes," Betty said. "That's supposed to be the footbridge near our house. I'm afraid I'm a long way from doing it justice."

"But you have some nice touches," Brooke told her. "Your cranberry bushes look quite realistic. And don't worry about the bridge for now. We'll focus on structures more in another lesson. Get your technique down for the grasses and other flora tonight. I'd say you have a good start."

"Thank you," Betty said, obviously pleased.

Brooke came to Mary's side. "I like your beach grass, Mary."

"Thanks. This is sort of what we see from our back patio, but not exactly." She laughed. "I guess it's a mishmash of what I know and what my brush does."

"That's okay," Brooke said. "Your tree looks a little odd though."

Mary frowned at it. "I think so too, but I wasn't sure how to fix it."

"Let me suggest a way to make the bark look mottled. Did you have a particular type of tree in mind?"

"I didn't," Mary confessed. "It's…you know…the required tree."

"I see," Brooke said with a chuckle. "Don't stress over the assignment. More than anything, I want you to have fun. Let's see if we can doctor that trunk a little. Load your brush with some of that nice dark brown you have there."

A couple of minutes later, while the tree still wasn't perfect, Mary was much more able to believe it *was* a tree, and she'd gleaned a little more knowledge on shading with her brush.

Brooke glanced at her watch. "All right, folks. Start looking for a stopping place and clean your brushes. We'll have refreshments in about ten minutes. Anyone need a little extra help now?"

Mary leaned over to admire her sister's painting. "That's quite good. I recognize the spot with no trouble."

Betty smiled at her as she flexed her fingers. "Thanks. Yours isn't bad either."

"It's not as good as yours. I think I did better last time, on the still life."

"Well, let's get some tea." Betty rose, and Mary went with her to the refreshment table.

Another of the students, Laura, was chatting with Brooke, while Linda poured out the tea and coffee.

"So when is the baby due?" Laura asked.

Before Brooke could answer, her mother said, "March 15. We can hardly wait!"

Laura gave a little laugh and looked at Brooke. "I guess that goes for you too?"

"Oh yes," Brooke said. "I'm counting down the days."

"Brooke is having another ultrasound next week," her mother said with an air of pride. "We'll get new pictures!"

Brooke looked slightly uncomfortable at this announcement. Mary wasn't sure whether Brooke didn't like having all her business broadcast, or if her mother's forwardness in general annoyed her, but Mary stepped forward and said, "Brooke, Betty and I had a very interesting outing this morning."

"Oh?" Brooke turned toward her eagerly.

"It has to do with art," Betty said. She gave Mary a complacent smile and stepped up to get her teacup.

Mary took that as approval from her sister and a go-ahead to tell Brooke about the paintings they had discovered. Unless she was mistaken, Betty would engage Linda in conversation, allowing Brooke to talk to her students without interruption.

"Yes, we were sorting through some things at my great-uncle's house in Provincetown, and we found several paintings his wife did sixty or seventy years ago."

"That's fascinating," Brooke said. "What sort of paintings?"

"Village scenes, very bright and active. Betty and I absolutely love them."

"So your great-aunt was an artist?"

"She was. I'd heard that before from my parents, but they didn't have any of her work. It was fun to finally see it."

"I'd love to take a look at them," Brooke said.

Mary nodded and shot a glance in her sister's direction. Betty and Linda were deep in a conversation about gardening, and Linda was expounding on what type of annuals she hoped to plant in her flower beds when the weather warmed up.

Mary smiled with satisfaction. She and Betty made a good team. Another student came to speak to Brooke, and this time, no one interrupted.

FOUR

——◆◆◆——

Betty had supper ready when Mary got home from the bookshop the next evening.

"It seemed like a beef stew night," Betty said, almost apologetically.

"It sure does—and you know I love beef stew. And biscuits! Did you use Mom's recipe?"

"I sure did. There's none better."

Mary ate in silence for a few minutes and then looked up. "I thought I'd call Jean later to talk to her about Aunt Maude."

"Perfect," Betty said. "I wonder how D.J.'s doing these days."

When they had finished eating and cleaned up the kitchen, Mary put through her call.

"Well, hi!" Jean's upbeat greeting made Mary smile.

Mary and Jean quickly caught up on each other's lives. Jean told Mary about her son, D.J., whose new technology job was going well. Mary was relieved—D.J. had struggled in his youth to find his niche, and the job sounded stable and fulfilling. Mary then told Jean the newest on her kids and grandchildren. Luke had recently score a big, game-winning goal in soccer, and Emma was testing at unusually high reading levels. Mary told Jean about Daisy, who was a typical teenager—social yet still insecure.

"Well, Mar," Jean said, "you remember—they get past this stage, although when you're in the thick of it, that's hard to believe."

"I know. I've explained that to Jack, but he's dubious." The cousins laughed.

"So what's up, Mary? Any particular reason for the call, or did you just feel like shooting the breeze?"

Mary smiled. "Actually, I do have something I wanted to chat about. Betty and I went out to Provincetown today. We weren't sure if you knew we inherited Uncle Lew's house."

"The lawyer didn't say as much, but I figured. Did you look at it yet?"

"Yes, and we found some interesting things in the attic."

Mary told her about the paintings and the other fascinating items they had found.

"Wow! I was glad I got the car, not the house, because I figured it would be a lot of work cleaning it out," Jean confessed. "But it sounds like you've got some fun stuff there."

After a bit more chatter, Jean said, "You know, I was offered a spot at a training seminar in Boston next week. My boss really wants me to take it and learn some cutting-edge bookkeeping software. I was dreading it, but if I could run down to Ivy Bay afterward…"

"Oh, that would be fantastic," Mary said. "We'd love to have you come."

"You talked me into it," Jean said. "I'll settle it with my boss in the morning. I'd love to see those paintings—and you and Betty, of course."

"We'll look forward to it," Mary said. When she had hung up, she found Betty in the living room and told her about Jean's planned visit.

"Wonderful," Betty said. "I hope she can stay over with us."

"She'll call when she's sure," Mary said. "Do you have any plans for tonight?"

"Just a new book, unless you have something else in mind."

"I wondered if you'd like to help me in my research on Uncle Lew and Aunt Maude. You've done so much family history I thought you might be able to find things I might not think of."

"Genealogy stuff?"

Mary shrugged. "Maybe. I don't really know, and that's the problem. I'd like to find Aunt Maude's friend Elle, but I'm not even sure where to begin on that. Maybe I need to know more about Aunt Maude first."

"*Hmm.* We could take a look at what I have on the Nelson family. That might be a good place to start."

A short time later, they sat down on the blue-and-white sofa in the living room, with Gus lolling on a cushion between them. Betty opened a notebook and handed it to Mary. "Here's the pedigree chart. Dad is here, and Gramps here. Since Uncle Lew was Gramps's brother but not our direct ancestor, he's not on this chart, but he's on the family group sheet for our great-grandparents."

She turned the pages until she came to a list with their great-grandfather's name at the top. She handed the notebook to Mary. Her great-grandmother was listed below her husband, and then their children, starting with Charles, who was the eldest, down to Lewis, the youngest, with several others between them. Betty had recently written in Uncle Lew's date and place of death.

"I see you have the date for his wedding to Maude." Mary studied the page. "Maude Price. Her maiden name?"

Betty nodded, took the binder back, and turned a couple more pages. "I don't have much on her or her family. But I do have a note that she grew up here in Ivy Bay."

"So they probably knew each other from childhood," Mary said. "And they were married in 1943. That's earlier than I expected."

"Me too. Uncle Lew must have been in the army already. He served in the European theater."

Mary smiled and turned the page. "Don't you just love finding out stuff like this? It makes me wish I'd paid more attention to the older people around us when I was young. Now, if Maude died in 1950, then she and Uncle Lew were married about seven years."

"But they had no children," Betty said, frowning at the page before her. "At least none that lived."

"It would have been fun to have more cousins." Mary stroked Gus's head and back. He began to purr. "I wonder when they moved to Provincetown."

"I'm guessing when he got home from the war, or soon after," Betty said.

"Yeah, maybe his business took him over there. He was an accountant, right? Maybe Ivy Bay had all the accountants they needed, but Provincetown was wide open, so he moved over there."

"The town was growing then. Lots of artists and little hotels and restaurants. Uncle Lew rented an office on the main street in Provincetown for a lot of years. Right up until he retired." Betty looked over at her. "You know, if Maude lived most of her life here, there are probably some older women in Ivy Bay who remember her."

"That's a great thought," Mary said. "I'll ask some of the ladies at church tomorrow. Some of them probably went to school with her." This puzzle, like so many before, was beginning to intrigue her.

———

Mary's efforts paid off when she questioned the older women in her Sunday school class. Irene Billings, who was ninety years old, recalled having known Maude personally.

"Sure, I knew Maude Price. I remember her wedding. It was right here in Grace Church. I attended with my younger sister."

After the class ended, Mary again spoke to Irene, hoping she could recall more details.

"She was a year behind me in school," Irene said, frowning as she searched her memory. "They got married in wartime, you know."

"Yes," Mary said. "It was in 1943."

"It kind of surprised me. Lew was a few years older than Maude, and they hadn't done much courting—not in school days, anyhow. I wondered if it was one of those hurry-up war weddings, where they tied the knot quick because he was going overseas."

"Could be," Mary said. "What was Aunt Maude like?"

"Kind of a dreamy girl. Pretty. And very artistic. I'd see her now and then down on the beach, sitting on a little campstool with an easel set up, just like the big-time artists that come here in summertime."

Mary nodded. "We were always told she was a good artist. Betty and I have inherited a few of her paintings from Uncle Lew. Do you know when they moved out to Provincetown?"

"*Hmm*, I don't know. After the war ended, I suppose."

"What did she look like?" Mary asked, unwilling to give up yet.

"She had the most beautiful natural blonde hair. Willowy figure." Irene smiled as she tucked her Bible under her arm and stood to walk to the auditorium. "Quite an impractical girl though. I don't think she did very well in school. She didn't seem to care about grades—more about her art."

That gave Mary a lot to think about. It did seem odd that Uncle Lew hadn't kept any of Aunt Maude's paintings out where he and other family members could enjoy them. But if they had parted in bitterness, as her letter to Elle suggested, perhaps it made sense that he had stuck them all in a corner of the attic where he didn't have to look at them. Or perhaps he felt guilty over their argument. When she died, his grief may have kept him from wanting to view her work constantly and be reminded of the past.

Mary looked forward to Jean's visit. She wanted Jean to go back to Provincetown with her and Betty, and to get those paintings home where she could examine them more closely. If they held clues to Aunt Maude's life during her brief marriage, Mary didn't want to miss them. Based on the letter they'd found, she wondered if the paintings might help them find Maude's friend Elle. And perhaps there was something special in the one she'd tagged for her friend. Mary was certain there was an intriguing story behind all of this. The more she thought about it, the more curious she got.

———

Mary and Rebecca had quite an influx of customers on Monday morning, almost as if all of Ivy Bay's mystery lovers had run out of reading material over the weekend. Mary loved talking to her customers and telling them about books she had read and enjoyed. She wished Rebecca's seven-year-old daughter, Ashley, could be there, instead of at school. Mary loved Ashley, and the little girl was a super salesperson when it came to children's books. Several customers asked about her and told Rebecca that they missed Ashley.

After lunch, the traffic was slower, and Mary did some reordering while Rebecca waited on the patrons and dusted the books and fixtures. Gus sprawled on the window seat, soaking up what sun flowed in.

About three o'clock, Mary asked Rebecca if she would mind being alone in the store for an hour or so. "I'd like to run over to the school for a bit."

"Go ahead," Rebecca told her. "I think the rush played out. I can certainly handle this."

Only one customer was in the store at the time, so Mary took her purse and a notebook, donned her woolen jacket, and drove to the public high school. She knew from experience that the most complete collection available of Ivy Bay High

School's yearbooks was housed in the school's library. While the public library had some of the volumes, for the earlier years, Mary was more likely to find what she wanted at the school.

Her neighbor Sherry Walinski sat at the desk inside the main office, where she worked as a secretary. She greeted Mary with a broad smile. "Good to see you, Mary. How can I help you today?"

"I'm here to look at some old school yearbooks in the library."

"Go on down," Sherry said, her green eyes twinkling. "I'm sure you know the way."

Mary was soon seated at an oak table with yearbooks spanning the years from 1938 to 1943 spread before her. Those would include the year Aunt Maude graduated, and probably Uncle Lew as well. If she got her wish, she might even find something about Maude's friend Elle.

She started with 1943, the year Lew and Maude were married, but didn't find either of them listed among the seniors. Next she tried 1942, with no luck there either, although she did see the portrait of one woman she now knew as a senior citizen.

In the 1941 book, she found Maude. Irene was right; the slender blonde girl had a wistful expression. It was easy for Mary to imagine her with a paintbrush in her hand.

Eagerly, she scanned the other photos of girls in Maude's class. Near the end of the section, she found what she was looking for: Elle Wetherly.

The girl had dark hair and eyes, and an elfish face. Just looking at her photo, Mary knew she liked that girl. In her portrait, Elle looked as though she could barely hold in a laugh. Mary imagined her as great fun to be around and an active, witty person. She had wondered if Elle was a nickname, but apparently not. Beneath the portrait was the caption "Elle P. Wetherly." Each of the girls wore a classical drape for the photos, so she couldn't tell anything about Elle from her clothing, but Mary leafed through the book, hoping to find other pictures of her.

She turned up a chorus group photo, but Elle was so tiny in it that Mary wouldn't have recognized her without the caption. On a page of candids, however, she found a shot of two girls eating lunch together, and though it wasn't labeled, she was sure they were Maude and Elle. Maude's shoulder-length blonde tresses and pensive smile were unmistakable. Beside her, Elle grinned and held up two fingers behind Maude's head for "bunny ears."

She wished she had thought to ask Irene Billings about Elle. If she remembered Maude, she probably remembered her best friend as well. When she mentioned Elle's name to the school librarian, however, she shook her head.

"I've only lived here about ten years. But there are probably older people in town who knew her."

Mary decided to drop in on Irene Billings before going back to the bookshop. Irene lived with her daughter's family, in a small house a block from the Seafarers' Hall. She was surprised to see Mary but seemed pleased.

"Why don't you sit down in the living room with Mama," Irene's daughter told Mary. "I could make you both some tea."

"I really shouldn't stop that long," Mary said, thinking of Rebecca alone at the store. "Maybe another time."

Irene was settled in a green plush recliner, and Mary took a seat on the sofa near the old woman.

"I've learned a little more about my great-aunt Maude," Mary began. "I found out that her best friend was named Elle Wetherly, and I wondered if you knew Elle."

"Oh, sure." Irene chuckled. "She was an imp, that girl. Everyone liked her, but she was always up to some mischief."

"She was in the chorus," Mary prompted.

"Was she? I don't remember. She was in a recital with me once though. We learned poems and pieces by heart and recited them. It was quite a to-do back then. We wore formal dresses, and the boys dressed up sharp in their Sunday suits. All the parents came to listen."

"I wish they had still done those things when I was in high school," Mary said. "My class did perform a play, but I think public speaking was overlooked during my school years."

Irene nodded. "It was one of the highlights of the year for us. I remember my piece was 'The Necklace,' by Guy de Maupassant. Very tragic. Everyone cried."

Mary smiled. "I know that one. The woman lost the borrowed necklace and worked for years to pay it off."

"That's the one," Irene said. "Then she found out it was a fake. I loved that story. Now the one Elle chose was of a different sort."

"You remember it?" Mary asked.

"*Hmm*, it was an O. Henry piece, I think. People laughed and laughed. She had a very comical way about her. I always thought she'd become an actress."

"Do you know what became of her?" Mary asked. "She doesn't live in Ivy Bay now, does she?"

"Oh no. She hasn't for ages."

"Did she go to Hollywood?"

Irene shook her head. "Not that I know of. I think she got married, but I can't remember who the fellow was. Anyhow, she moved away." She chuckled. "Haven't thought about her in years. She was very smart. Did I say that? She could have done anything she wanted, I suppose."

"She and Maude were the best of friends, weren't they?"

"Inseparable. Elle stood up for Maude in her wedding— did I tell you that?"

"No, but it's good to know. Was Elle married then?"

"I don't think so. Still Wetherly, I believe, but my memory's not what it used to be. I almost think Elle married someone from away."

Mary thanked her and headed back to the store, mulling over the new bits of information she had gleaned. She had learned enough about the two girls, Maude and Elle, that she wanted to know the end of the story.

The letter Aunt Maude had written to Elle seemed to be a pivotal item. When had Maude written it? Where did it fall in regard to her death? Did she write the letter and hide it in the back of the painting shortly before she died? And how did Maude die? There seemed to be no indication in the guest book from the funeral. And why was the painting still in Uncle Lew's attic? Why had Maude's dearest friend never received her gift?

When Mary got back to the bookshop, Rebecca was helping the only customer in the store. Mary took out the brief letter to Elle and read it again. A niggling thought had suggested that perhaps Elle had helped Maude disappear in order to escape an unhappy marriage to Uncle Lew, then covered her tracks for her friend. But the letter indicated otherwise. It was all Mary had to go on, but according to that brief note, Maude didn't tell Elle where she was going, or with whom, even though Elle still seemed to have been a close friend.

She lingered over the line, "He is the only person I can trust." Why wasn't Elle counted as one whom Maude could trust? If she was such a good friend, wouldn't she have helped Maude in a time of dire need?

Mary could hardly wait to get home, even though she loved her cozy bookshop. As soon as she could, she cashed out the day's receipts and locked the door. The first thing she did at home, after greeting Betty and hanging up her coat, was to rush upstairs to get the old guest book from Aunt Maude's funeral. She sat down at her desk and went carefully through the names. When she was certain Elle Wetherly had not signed the roster, she closed the book with a sigh. Nobody named Wetherly had attended the service, and no one with a first name of Elle.

If Maude and Elle had remained friends, why hadn't Elle attended her funeral? And why hadn't Elle at some point received the painting Maude had left for her, and according to the letter, had promised her? Something must have happened, and it seemed as though it tore those friends apart. Whatever it was, Mary was determined to uncover the truth.

FIVE

J ean joined Mary and Betty for supper on Friday, after driving down from Boston in a rental car.

"I'm glad I went to the seminar," Jean admitted. "I learned a lot, and it could really make a difference when there's a chance for a promotion in the office."

"That's great," Betty said. "We're so glad you decided to do it—and come here too."

After supper, Mary showed Jean the pictures she had taken of Aunt Maude's paintings, and Jean had brought along a couple of photos from her family album to share. They settled down in the living room to discuss them.

"Here's a picture of Aunt Maude." Jean handed her the first one. "I didn't have many."

"Neither did we," Mary said. "I did find her senior picture in her school yearbook though."

She looked at the photo, which was a black-and-white snapshot of Aunt Maude outside the Provincetown house.

"It says on the back when it was taken," Jean said.

Mary turned it over. "Our new place, July '46. Well, I guess that settles that question." She handed the picture to Betty.

"Here's their wedding photo."

Betty leaned in to look with her. "I wish we had some color photos."

"These are too early for color, I think," Jean replied. "At least it wasn't common yet."

Next, she produced a picture of Uncle Lew in his army uniform—a handsome young man. Mary traced the lines of his face and recognized the elderly man she remembered.

The next photo, of Uncle Lew standing beside a 1970s sedan, was a color snapshot. Uncle Lew's hair was a medium brown. He had been gray for many years, and Mary enjoyed seeing these glimpses of the younger man.

The car Jean had inherited was much newer than the one in the photo, and Mary turned to her cousin, curious about the bequest.

"Are you going to keep Uncle Lew's car?"

"I don't think so. I got a new one last year, and I like it. I'm thinking about whether to give it to D.J. or just sell it. He doesn't really need one right now, but we'll see."

Jean went with Mary and Betty to Provincetown the following morning, prepared to make a day of it, with several cartons folded up in the trunk of Betty's car and a roll of packing tape.

"I do want to talk to some more of Uncle Lew's neighbors," Mary said to Betty. "You don't mind, do you?"

"No, but I'd like to finish our sorting today, so we don't have to come back again."

"I'll help," Jean said. "We can start with the nearest neighbors."

"Thanks," Mary told her. "Bets, I'll go to the house beyond Tom Fuller's. I want to find some people who lived here when Aunt Maude was alive, if possible. Do you want to take the one on the other side?"

"All right," Betty said.

"I'll go with you, Betty, if you don't mind," Jean told her.

"If they knew Uncle Lew, don't forget to ask if they knew Aunt Maude. And even if they didn't, ask if they ever heard how she died."

"You're optimistic, aren't you?" Betty asked. "Remember, Aunt Maude only lived here about four years."

Mary shrugged. "I know, but that's how I learn things— by asking lots of questions."

"We'll do our best." Betty parked in Uncle Lew's driveway. The Fuller house showed no sign of activity.

"I'll meet you back here in ten minutes or so," Mary said, heading resolutely down the sidewalk, which was now clear of snow. She didn't want to tire Betty out on this quest for information about Aunt Maude, but she probably wouldn't have as good a chance to talk to the neighbors for a while.

The woman who answered the door of the neat white Cape beyond the Fullers' house smiled at her curiously. "Hi."

"I'm Mary Fisher, and I'm a great-niece of Lewis Nelson. He used to own the house over there, on the other side of the Fullers."

"Oh, sure. Come on in." The woman opened her storm door and beckoned Mary inside. "I'm Pam Schuller."

"Thank you." Mary stepped in and shut the storm door firmly behind her. "I just wondered if you knew Uncle Lew. My sister and I inherited the house, and we're trying to find out more about him and our Aunt Maude."

"Aunt Maude?" Mrs. Schuller, who had honey-blonde hair with a few streaks of gray, frowned. "I don't think I ever met her. That was Lew's wife?"

"Yes, but she probably died before you were born," Mary said. "In 1950, to be exact."

"Oh." Mrs. Schuller laughed. "Yeah, that was before my time. But, hey! My mother might remember her. She and Dad lived here then. In fact, I grew up here, and I've known Mr. Nelson since I was a kid. My husband and I moved back here with Mom about eight years ago, after my father died."

"Does your mother still live here?"

"Yeah, she's in the living room. Would you like to meet her?"

Mary's excitement stirred. "I'd love to." Soon she was seated next to the older woman. "My sister and our cousin and I are going to do some work at Uncle Lew's house this morning, so I can't stay long," she said after the introductions, "but I would like very much to find someone who remembers my Aunt Maude."

"Oh my, yes," the white-haired Mrs. Adams said. "That was a long time ago. She was a painter."

"That's right," Mary said, trying to restrain her glee at finding someone who remembered. "Can you tell me what she was like?"

"She and I were both young brides. I had my oldest daughter, Nancy, and I remember her coming over to see the

baby. I liked her. My husband and hers didn't get along so
well though."

"Oh? Why not?"

"Ralph didn't take to Lew Nelson. They couldn't seem to
agree on anything—politics, religion, or what kind of car they
liked. Oil and water, those two. And I probably shouldn't say
it, but your uncle had a temper."

Mary tried not to show her surprise at Mrs. Adams's
frankness. "Did he? It's all right—you can tell me. I'm not
going to be upset."

"Well, I don't think he was the easiest man to live with."

As the old woman talked, Mary tried to imagine the two
young couples trying to get along in the neighborhood that
was probably much more sparsely populated at that time. This
was part of her family heritage. She had grown up loving Uncle
Lew simply because he was part of the family, but she realized
now she hadn't known him well. Hearing other people's
perspectives on him was a bit deflating. Learning more about
Lew and Maude had been a pleasant distraction to this point,
but she found that in order to gain a better understanding, she
needed to learn how Aunt Maude died. She found herself half
listening to Mrs. Adams's comments on Lew and planning
how she could politely turn the conversation to Maude's
death. Maybe a direct approach was best.

"Do you remember when Maude died? I'm curious about
that."

Mrs. Adams waved her hand through the air. "Oh, I could
tell you a story."

Ten minutes later, Mary took her leave, wishing she
could talk longer with the elderly woman, but knew she'd

already stayed longer than she should. She hoped Betty and Jean weren't standing in the cold, waiting for her.

To her relief, her sister and Jean were heading toward her, walking slowly along the sidewalk. Mary hurried toward them.

"Hi! Sorry I took so long," she called as they neared one another.

"It's all right," Betty said. "We found two people who said they knew Uncle Lew, but Aunt Maude was already gone when they moved here."

"I guess we should expect that." Even so, Mary was disappointed.

"I asked about Elle too," Betty said, "but nobody recognized the name."

Mary nodded. "She didn't live here, so I wouldn't expect them to. Oh well."

"One fellow had vague memories of things he'd heard about Maude," Jean said. "He told us he thought she drowned when she was quite young. That's the best we can do for you. Sorry."

"Drowned?" Mary frowned. "That might fit with a tragic death. But still, wouldn't we have known that?"

"I never heard Dad say anything about a drowning," Betty said firmly.

"My folks didn't either." Jean shook her head. "Mary, did you learn anything?"

"Sort of. I chatted with an elderly lady who moved in about the same time as Lew and Maude. She and Maude were friends. But she told me Uncle Lew had a bad temper, and her husband didn't like him."

"So now we're hearing the nitty-gritty," Betty said. They walked up the driveway toward Uncle Lew's house.

"Hold on to your hat," Mary said. "She also said her husband thought maybe Uncle Lew killed Aunt Maude, but she didn't believe it."

Betty's jaw dropped. "You're joking."

"Sort of. I mean, she laughed about it, but I had to wonder if she didn't think there was a grain of truth to it. She said Aunt Maude up and disappeared one day."

Jean stared at her. "But there was a funeral."

Mary nodded. "Yeah, she remembered that. She didn't go to it. She had a new baby then and a couple of toddlers."

"But she didn't say Aunt Maude drowned?" Betty asked.

"No. I asked her if she knew what happened, and she said she didn't. She thought it was some kind of an accident. But her daughter told me Mrs. Adams's memory is on the fritz now."

They had climbed the porch steps as they talked. Betty took the key from her purse and opened the front door. "The consensus among the people Jean and I talked to was that Uncle Lew was a decent neighbor."

"Yeah, I'm thinking maybe Mr. Adams had a political argument or something with him, and they never got along," Mary said.

"Still, you don't slander someone like that, saying he murdered his wife." Betty's face was troubled.

"I wish Mr. Adams was still alive," Mary said. "I'd love to know whether he was serious when he said it."

"Well, are you two ready to go to work?" Betty asked more brightly.

"Whenever you are," Jean replied.

Mary hesitated. "If you don't mind, I'd like to step across the street. Mrs. Adams and her daughter told me about a gentleman over there who might remember Aunt Maude."

"Okay," Betty said. "I'm going to get started in the kitchen. I'll make some tea, and when you come back, we'll have a cup before we head up to the attic."

"Sounds good."

Mary walked briskly to the house Pam Schuller had indicated. The man who opened the door to her knock had once been tall but now stood hunched over, blinking at her from beneath full white eyebrows.

"Hello, Mr. Bentley. I'm Lew Nelson's niece."

Everyone in the neighborhood knew the Nelson name. Once Mary had made known her mission, the old man invited her in. The small house smelled of tobacco and coffee.

"Do you want to sit down?" Mr. Bentley asked.

"No, thank you," Mary said. "My sister and I plan to do a lot of cleaning over at Uncle Lew's house. As I mentioned, I just wanted to see if you could tell me anything about Aunt Maude."

He nodded sagely. "That one was pretty. A good painter too. I remember she used to sit on the beach and paint."

"Do you know where any of her paintings are now?" Mary asked. Perhaps one of the neighbors had invested in Maude's work.

But Mr. Bentley shook his head. "She used to sell them to the tourists. You might check with the galleries."

"Thanks. I'll do that." Mary eyed him earnestly. "Do you remember what happened to Maude?"

"Oh, she died. Quite young too." He cocked his head to one side. "But how? Now, that's the question."

"What do you mean?"

"There were stories."

"What kind of stories?"

"First, they said she drowned." Mr. Bentley shrugged. "Then she didn't. Or they weren't sure. I can't remember the details, but people wondered about that for a long time."

"She's buried in the cemetery here in town," Mary said.

"Ah."

The way he said it made Mary shiver. "Well, I suppose my sister is waiting for me. Thank you, Mr. Bentley."

She left the small, gray house and hurried back to Uncle Lew's. She wished she had time to go to one of the older newspapers in town and search their archives. She might find Aunt Maude's obituary or some small news brief about her death.

But time was fleeting, and she and Betty must take care of things at the house, and Jean had to drive to Boston that evening to catch her plane back to Chicago. They had a lot to do, and she wouldn't ask Betty and Jean for more time. But she would pursue that drowning rumor. Maybe she could find something online later.

"You're just in time," Betty said when she entered Uncle Lew's kitchen. "The tea's been steeping for a few minutes."

"Oh, good. I'm ready for it." The house wasn't as cold as it had been on their first foray, and Mary unzipped her jacket. "Find anything good?"

"As far as tea goes? I'm using the chai blend I brought, but it's Aunt Maude's teapot."

Mary spotted it on the counter—a white china pot with ivy vines twining around it. "Very pretty. Hand painted?"

"I think so. I wondered if she got one with ivy because she lived in Ivy Bay. Lots of people there use ivy in their decorations, you know."

"Could be," Mary said, as Jean brought a sugar bowl and a container of powdered creamer to the table.

"Maybe she even painted it herself. I think I may keep it," Betty said.

"You should keep anything you like, for whatever reason," Mary said. "That's my philosophy when it comes to mementos. That goes for you too, Jean."

"I have a collection of teapots already." Betty had set out three cups and saucers, and Jean filled them with tea. "But I do like it."

Mary smiled and took the cup with daffodils on the side. She carried it to the table, where Betty had left a plastic bag of gingersnaps, and sat down. Betty brought her cup, ornamented with violets, and took a chair opposite her, and Jean, whose cup had blue-and-white forget-me-nots, sat down at one side of the table.

"Are you ready to go up to the attic after we're done here?" Mary asked.

"Yes, I can't wait for Jean to see the paintings and get the full effect. But I'm afraid we might get bogged down there." Betty dipped a cookie in her tea and bit off the edge.

"It's really hard not to get distracted when you're cleaning out an attic," Jean agreed.

"Where do you think we're most apt to find things we want?" Mary asked. "Other than the paintings, I mean."

Betty considered her question. "Well...we did go through his desk already. All right, let's start with the attic first, but we need to set a time limit up there. We don't want to be exhausted and still have to deal with the rest of the house."

Mary and Jean agreed, and when they had finished their tea break, they set to work. They had already decided to get anything they wanted today and let the rest go, without looking back. That meant Mary had to make sure they found every significant item within the next few hours. After today, they would leave everything in an estate-sale broker's hands.

When Jean saw the paintings, her delight was evident on her face. "Oh, how wonderful!"

Mary looked at Betty, wishing they had discussed whether they might offer one of the paintings to their cousin. She decided not to mention it now, but they could talk about it later, when Jean wasn't with them.

Two hours later, they finished in the attic. Mary took the paintings down the stairs one by one. Betty set aside a hatbox and an old watering can. Mary found a set of bronze bookends and a box of antique children's books she decided to take to the bookshop. Jean rescued a few picture postcards and a small ironstone platter. The rest of the attic findings, they agreed, could be sold.

They made short work of the sparsely furnished bedrooms on the second floor and carried their treasures and two bags of trash down to the ground level.

"Time to break out the sandwiches," Mary said. "It's half past noon."

They ate their lunch in the kitchen and discussed selling the house. Betty had located a Provincetown real estate agent on the recommendation of a friend, and the agent had agreed to meet them at the house at two o'clock.

"If we can finish our sorting before she gets here, that would be good," Betty said. "We need to be out of here by three so Jean can make the airport on time."

Mary nodded. "I'll be ready to go by then. It shouldn't take long to show her over the house. You should stay down here and rest though. I'll take her upstairs. She can start showing the place as soon as the sale's been held to clear out the contents."

"The weather might put a damper on the sale plans," Betty noted.

"It could. Do you think we should wait a couple of months for spring weather? More people would come out for it if we waited until May—or at least April."

Betty shrugged. "True, but I'd rather be done with it. Wouldn't you?"

She looked so wistful that Mary readily agreed. "We don't expect to make much money from selling the furniture and things, anyway. I don't think it makes much difference—and the seller will haul away whatever's left for us. That's part of the deal."

"You know," Jean said, reaching for a cookie, "I'm glad I got to come and help you two today, but I'm glad it's not me having to handle all this too."

After they finished eating, they dove into the work once more. Mary grew selective as she sorted the books in the living room, forcing herself to take only ones she herself would read or that fit her mystery-bookshop theme.

On one of the lower shelves, she found an album. "Look, Bets! Finally—a photo album."

Betty and Jean came over to watch as Mary opened it. Inside, they found a few dozen family photos, including snapshots of themselves as girls and a few of their parents and Cousin Jean's family.

"There don't seem to be any of Aunt Maude," Betty said mournfully. "I'm almost convinced she did leave him. It's like he tried to get rid of every trace of her."

"So sad," Mary murmured as she closed the book. "I'll take this home."

"I'm almost done in the pantry," Jean said. "I've got one more shelf to scrub down."

"And I left this bookcase until last," Mary said. "After this, I'm done."

"Let me know if you find anything older than us." Betty went to the side wall and took down the embroidered motto. "I think I'll take this, for sentiment's sake."

By two, they were finished, and Mary had packed the car with everything they intended to keep. The agent arrived punctually, and in less than half an hour, they headed home. When Betty stopped at the collectibles shop owned by the couple who would oversee the estate sale, Mary went in to leave them a key to the house.

"There," she said when she got back into the car. "If the weather looks good, they'll do it two weeks from Saturday. But they'll call first and let us know."

"Great." Betty put the car in gear. "So that's that."

"Yes," Mary said, but she knew that *wasn't* that. She had too many unanswered questions.

SIX

————◆◆◆————

I really don't know where we'll put them." Betty frowned as she looked at the five paintings that Mary had stood up around the wall in the living room. Jean had gone to the airport in her rental car, and the sisters were left to find places for the treasures they'd brought home.

"There's certainly not room in here." Mary looked about at the artwork Betty had chosen so carefully for this room. All were paintings or textiles from the Federalist period, to complement the architecture and furniture. While Aunt Maude's paintings were well executed, they didn't blend in here. "I wonder if one or two could go in the sunroom?"

"Maybe." Betty hesitated. "Or you could take them upstairs."

"But you wouldn't be able to see them." Betty infrequently climbed the stairs because of her arthritis, and Mary had observed how the efforts she'd made at Uncle Lew's house had worn her out a bit.

"You could bring one down if we wanted to examine it closely. Oh, I don't know. I really love this one." Betty pointed to the first painting they'd uncovered.

"That's the one that says 'To Elle.' Maybe we should keep it down here, where it's more accessible, while we try to find out more about Elle Wetherly." Mary arched her eyebrows and waited for her sister's decision. This house was Betty's domain, and Mary would accept whatever verdict made her happy.

Betty nodded. "I think that's a good idea. We could even replace that seascape in the sunroom for a while, if you like. I think it would fit nicely in there. We can store the other painting in the hall closet."

"Great. I'll wrap it first," Mary said.

"Oh, and if you want to hang the others upstairs, go ahead," Betty said. "The guest room has that picture rail I had installed, and you can hang as many paintings as you want without damaging the walls."

"Perfect." Mary picked up the largest frame and made her way upstairs. She left it in the guest room and went back down for another.

Betty was headed toward her bedroom but turned back. "If you'll forgive me, I think I'll take a nap."

"You go right ahead," Mary said. "After I take these upstairs, I'm going to the shop."

Since Gus had been home alone for most of the day, she decided to take him with her. Occasionally she left him home with Betty, but Gus seemed to like variety, and he considered the bookshop his kingdom.

When they arrived, Rebecca was checking out a customer, and another waited with her arms full of books. Three other people were browsing the shelves. Mary nodded and smiled at Rebecca and hurried to the back room to leave her coat and release Gus. She jumped into helping the customers, and half an hour passed before she had a moment to talk to her assistant.

"How did it go today?" Rebecca asked.

"Very well. We finished sorting, and we brought home everything we want to keep. I'm afraid Betty is exhausted though."

"That's too bad. But you got your aunt's paintings out of the house?"

Mary nodded. She had told Rebecca about their find and how badly she wanted to learn more about Aunt Maude and her artwork, as well as the circumstances of her death. "I had hoped to go to the library today, but it's too late now."

Rebecca glanced at the clock. "Yes, I think you're right."

"I'll do it another day."

The bell on the door jingled, and two women from Mary's church came in.

"Hello, ladies!" She enjoyed catching up on her friends' activities and then directed them to the latest mysteries in the genres they preferred. One liked British mysteries, especially of the "locked room" variety, and the other preferred cozy mysteries in American settings. Mary was able to help them both find new reading material.

It wasn't until Monday that she got to the public library. She toyed with the idea of reserving a full day to go back to Provincetown to pursue her inquiries, but it made sense to see what she could find in Ivy Bay first. After all, Maude and Elle had grown up here.

At the library, she strode directly to the librarian's desk. "Hi, Victoria."

Victoria Pickerton looked up from her computer screen and smiled. "Hi, Mary. How are things at the bookshop?" She stood and came out from behind the desk. Sunlight beaming down from the skylight overhead gleamed on her short, dark hair.

"Going well," Mary said. "I hope you can help me with something fun."

"I'd love to."

Mary smiled. "I knew you would. I'm looking for information about my great-aunt, Maude Nelson. She died in 1950, I believe in the town of Provincetown. There seems to be some question as to how she died."

"Oh my. Well, we can try the old newspapers we have on file, and it sounds like the Nexis service might be a good place to start. That gives us access to newspaper files nationwide, you know."

"Yes, I was thinking of that. I hope it will let me look at Provincetown newspapers from 1950."

"Let's take a look."

Mary followed Victoria to one of the computers available for public use. Since she had the date of Aunt Maude's funeral service from the guest book, they looked for that first. Mary found a notice of the service, held in a Provincetown funeral home. On a hunch, she asked Victoria for a Provincetown phone book and turned to the yellow pages.

"Hooray," she said softly.

"Find something?" Victoria asked.

"This funeral home was a family-run business, and it's still in operation." She copied the telephone number. "I heard a rumor from some of the neighbors that Aunt Maude drowned, but they didn't have any details, and I wasn't sure they were right about that. No one in the family ever told Betty or me that she'd drowned."

"You can look for news articles about drownings, and maybe find her obituary," Victoria suggested.

"Both good ideas. Thanks."

Back at the computer, Mary continued browsing the old Provincetown newspapers, starting a few weeks before the date of the funeral service. Though she kept an eagle eye on the obituary column, Aunt Maude's name didn't turn up. However, she did find a brief notice stating that a body had washed ashore in Ivy Bay. She checked the date of the newspaper. It was from August of 1950. The timing was about right, but apparently this drowning had taken place in Ivy Bay, not Provincetown. Curious, she closed the Nexis program and went to the room where the old Ivy Bay newspapers were archived. She might find more details here than in the computerized issues.

She started with the date from the Provincetown article and worked backward. Sure enough, in a paper published a few days earlier, she spotted a news story about an unidentified body washing ashore just east of Ivy Bay's boat landing. Carefully, Mary searched the next issues of the same newspaper. Another brief story appeared a couple of days later, indicating the local police had not yet identified the body, but were trying to match its characteristics with missing persons reports.

In the precomputer days, that would have been much more difficult than in modern times, Mary mused. Still, Maude had grown up in Ivy Bay, where the body appeared. Wouldn't someone recognize her? She supposed that depended on the body's condition when it was found. The article didn't give many details, except to confirm that it was a woman's body.

Mary stared down at the bleak announcement and swallowed hard. The whole idea was rather horrific. Could this have been Aunt Maude's end? If so, how did her drowning come about? She remembered the letter to Elle that Maude had hidden in the painting. Had the "only person she could trust" not protected Maude?

She shook off the chill that had crept over her. Time to get back to the bookshop and give Rebecca a break. She'd been leaving her assistant alone far too much lately. If business was slow, she could call the funeral home from there. And when she had time, she would sit and think this through. There had to be a logical thread that would tie up all the loose ends in this morbid tale.

After lunch, at a time when no customers were in the shop, she called the number for the funeral home in Provincetown. The woman who answered put her through to the funeral director.

"That service would have been conducted by my father," he said. "I was only a toddler then."

"I understand. Do you still have records from that time?" Mary asked.

"Yes, of course. I can look it up for you. What exactly did you wish to know?"

"Anything you can tell me about the funeral, and the— the care of the body, if that's possible."

"I'll see what I can find." He took her number and called her back in a surprisingly short time. "As I thought, that client was handled by my father. The arrangements were made by Lewis Nelson, the husband of the deceased."

"Yes, he was my great-uncle," Mary said.

"Apparently that was more of a memorial service than a funeral," the man told her.

Mary frowned. "Do you mean…there was no body?"

"That's right. My father's notes say Mrs. Nelson had drowned, and her husband wanted a memorial, to bring closure for the family. So my father never had the body here at the home."

"Oh my." Mary's stomach plummeted. She truly hadn't expected that, and she didn't know what to say, except "Thank you very much."

For the rest of the afternoon, as she worked about the store, Mary found her thoughts going back to Aunt Maude. When Joe and Iris Drury, a married couple slightly older than her, came into the shop, she saw an opportunity to get the opinion of someone who'd been on the spot. Mr. and Mrs. Joseph Drury Sr. had signed the funeral guest book.

After greeting the couple warmly and asking them how they'd enjoyed the last batch of mysteries they'd bought, Mary turned the conversation to Aunt Maude.

"Betty and I found the old guest book from her funeral in 1950," she said. "Joe, your parents went to the service and signed the book."

"How about that," Joe said, shaking his head. "I was only a kid then. I'm sure I didn't go."

"Do you remember Lew and Maude Nelson at all?" Mary asked.

His forehead wrinkled as he considered that. "Don't think so."

"They had moved to Provincetown. I guess it would be odd if you did. I was hoping I could find someone who was there and could tell me about the memorial service."

"Mom and Pop are long gone, I'm afraid. I could ask my sister though." Joe's expression brightened. "She was a teenager. It's possible she knew your aunt and uncle. She might even have gone along with our folks. But she probably stayed home with me and my little sister."

"I'd appreciate it if you'd ask her," Mary said. "Another odd thing happened that year."

"What's that?" Joe asked.

"A body washed up on the beach here that summer, beyond the boat landing."

"I remember that," Joe said immediately.

"So do I," Iris chimed in. "All the kids swarmed down there to watch the ambulance take the body away. My mother wouldn't let me go."

"I went." Joe shuddered. "It was pretty grisly, and I've never forgotten it."

"Everybody in town talked about it for a while," Iris said. "Until the next bit of news."

"Do you want me to call my sister about your aunt's funeral?" Joe asked.

"If you don't mind."

Iris smiled as she scanned the new book releases on the front table. "Mary, talking about that drowning thing brought back memories. It sounds like a plot as twisted as some of the books we read. You ought to write a mystery about it."

Mary chuckled. "Maybe someday, but don't hold your breath." The truth was, she had a partly written manuscript in the bottom drawer of her desk at home, but she wasn't sure she would ever finish it. Her attempts were sporadic at best, and she was sure her story would never be half as good as those of the authors she loved.

She chatted a little more with the Drurys, and they chose a new book by a favorite author and an older Dick Francis novel they'd never read. Other patrons came into the shop. As she and Rebecca waited on them, Mary kept turning over Maude's story in her mind.

If the drowning victim was not Aunt Maude, why had Uncle Lew held a memorial service? And if it was, why had the remains not been sent to the funeral home?

Not too long ago, she'd read a novel about a woman who staged her own death in order to avoid being charged with a crime. Was it possible Maude might have done that—set up a scenario that made it look as though she had died in order to escape a loveless marriage in a way that would keep her husband from looking for her?

Another possibility occurred to her: What if Aunt Maude had taken advantage of the tragedy as a way to explain her disappearance? But still, the note to Elle had shown no indication of that, or the possibility that Maude would try to make it appear as though she had died.

Also, if that drowned woman hadn't been Aunt Maude, who was it? One person in town could probably find the answer for her.

She strode toward the counter and the phone sitting on it, but it rang before she could place her call.

"Mary Fisher?" an elderly woman asked in a sharp voice that reminded Mary of her junior high civics teacher's.

"Yes."

"This is Anita Platt. I'm Joe Drury's sister. He asked me to call you if I remembered Maude Nelson's funeral."

"Oh yes. Thank you very much," Mary said. "Did you attend the memorial service in Provincetown?"

"No, I babysat that day, as usual, but Joe said you were curious about that body they found near the boat landing."

"That's right," Mary said. "It happened within a month of Aunt Maude's funeral, and I wondered if she might possibly have been the drowning victim."

"Nah, I don't think so," Mrs. Platt said. "My mother talked about it—seems like they thought it was her, but it turned out to be somebody else."

"Do you remember who?" Mary asked.

"Nope. But the police chief could probably tell you."

"I've been thinking that very thing. Thank you very much for calling."

Mary hung up determined to see Chief McArthur soon. The chief was a childhood friend of hers, from when Mary and Betty had summered in Ivy Bay with their grandparents. He was a couple of years older than Mary and had been the chief for more than thirty years. If anyone could help her solve the riddle of the unidentified drowning victim, Chief McArthur could.

As the business day drew to a close, she double-checked the dates she'd accumulated concerning Aunt Maude. Her memorial service had been held about three weeks after the body washed ashore. Was the timing coincidental? And were the drowning rumors she'd heard from Uncle Lew's neighbors based on this tragedy, even if the unidentified body wasn't really Aunt Maude's? Or had she drowned as well? The funeral director's assertion that Maude's body was absent from her memorial service troubled Mary. Maude's letter to Elle had said she was leaving her husband. Did she try to do that and come to a tragic end? Then where was her body? Wasn't it lying in the Provincetown cemetery?

The whole thing unsettled her, and she didn't know if she'd be able to sleep tonight. As Rebecca locked the front door and turned the sign to Closed, Mary called the police station.

"I know it's late in the day," she told the officer on the desk, "but I wondered if I might possibly see Chief McArthur."

"Hold on, Mrs. Fisher. I'll ask him."

A moment later, Chief McArthur's voice boomed in her ear. "Mary, how can I help you?"

"I'd like to discuss an old case with you, Chief. It's connected to my family, and I admit it's got me a bit muddled. I don't want to bother you or keep you from going home to dinner, but... could I come over to the station and discuss it with you?"

"Come on over," Chief McArthur said. "My schedule is flexible."

Mary quickly cashed out the day's receipts and prepared her bank deposit for the next morning. A few minutes later, she left the shop with Gus curled on the cushion in his carrier.

"You can't go into the police station," she told him, "but I should only be a few minutes." Even so, she left the car's heater running at medium, so that Gus wouldn't be cold in his carrier.

Once admitted to Chief McArthur's private office, Mary quickly gave him the bare bones of her investigation.

He frowned and leaned back in his chair. "You say this happened in 1950? That's way before my time."

"Mine too," Mary said. "It's the year I was born. But I thought there would surely be some records somewhere about this body washing ashore in town. A police report, surely, and maybe an autopsy report? I'd really like to settle the question once and for all of whether that drowning victim was Maude Nelson."

"We've been busy this week, but when I get a chance, I'll try to look up the records for you."

"Thanks. I guess I hoped it would be on your computer and you'd have immediate access."

"We're getting there. Believe it or not, there are still a lot of old records that haven't been computerized. I've tried to get funding for several years to pay a clerk to do some of that work, but the budget keeps getting trimmed by the town council."

"Ah, yes. Politics."

Chief McArthur shrugged. "I don't blame them for trying to keep taxes down, but I don't like to see my department getting the short end of the stick. Anyway, I'll look into this for you as soon as I can."

"Thanks a lot." Mary stood and pulled on her gloves. The chief had helped her several times before, and she knew he would keep his word. Now to get home and see how Betty was doing.

A blast of cold air hit her as she left the police station. Tonight would be a good night to stay in. And maybe a good night to dig into Uncle Lew's papers. Did the boxes they'd brought home from Provincetown hold clues to Aunt Maude's mysterious death? Mary was determined to find out what had happened to her, no matter where the evidence led.

SEVEN

————◆◆◆————

After supper, the sisters sat down together in the comfortable living room. Betty sat with her legs elevated and a heating pad nestled over her right knee while she read the next novel her book club would discuss. Mary settled on the sofa with a box of Uncle Lew's old papers and sorted them on the coffee table.

She'd chosen the box with the oldest papers—one they'd found in the attic, not the things from his desk. Among a plethora of receipts and bank statements, she found the record of his discharge from the navy and tax returns dating back to the late 1940s. Mary glanced over them with interest. The forms didn't give as much information as a modern tax return would, but she put them in order and compared the yearly reports. Uncle Lew's income from his accounting business seemed very modest, though she realized modern inflation helped make those numbers look even smaller than they were.

"Other income," she said under her breath.

"What's that?" Betty looked up from her book.

"Oh, in 1948 and 1949, Uncle Lew and Aunt Maude reported some other income, besides what he earned in the accounting business."

"Maybe that was from Aunt Maude's artwork."

"That's what I was thinking, but how can I find out?" Mary began rummaging through the piles of receipts, and Betty went back to her reading.

The stacks on the coffee table grew larger as Mary sorted the items from the box. At last she held up a yellow slip of paper in triumph.

"Look at this! It's from the Ivy Bay Gallery, and it has Aunt Maude's name at the top." She rose and took the paper over to Betty's recliner.

"Two paintings, $140. Are you sure she's selling, not buying?"

"Yes, look—it's a consignment statement."

"Well, that seems pretty good for the time. I mean, for an unknown artist," Betty said.

"I think so too, especially considering that Uncle Lew's pay for the accounting business was less than a hundred dollars a week. This little bonus in August of 1947 would have given them quite a boost."

Mary set the receipt aside and turned back to the box, hoping she would find more indicators that Maude's paintings were selling during the period of her marriage. When she reached the bottom of the box, she held up the meager pile so Betty could see it.

"I've found receipts for five sold paintings over a three-year period. I suppose there may have been more."

"Does that box cover everything up to Aunt Maude's death?" Betty asked.

"I don't think so. The 1950 tax return isn't in here."

"Maybe it's in another box."

Mary gazed down at the sheaf of papers in her hand. "It would be nice to see that one. I'm curious how Uncle Lew handled it that year."

"He was an accountant, so I'm sure he filed it properly," Betty said.

"Me too. I just wonder..." Mary shuffled through the painting receipts again. "These are all from the Ivy Bay Gallery. But Maude had moved to Provincetown by then. I wonder if she also placed paintings in galleries over there, or if she only displayed her work here in Ivy Bay."

"Maybe Mr. Willoughby can give you some guidance." Betty moved her bookmark and laid her book down. "He's owned the gallery for quite a while, though he's not old enough to have owned it in 1950."

"I'll ask him. And I'll go through Uncle Lew's check registers." Mary reached for the stack of little booklets. "I may be able to tell when they deposited money other than his regular salary."

"Of course, he owned his own business, and he might not have paid himself every week," Betty said. "Business practices weren't always the same back then as we know them today."

"True." Mary spent a little more time on the financial documents and found a couple of receipts for which she couldn't identify the purpose, but nothing else that definitely pertained to Aunt Maude's art. At last she put the irrelevant papers back in the box and stacked the ones she might want to reference again into a neat pile.

She rose and stretched her arms and legs. "I'm ready for some tea. How about you?"

Betty had resumed reading, but she looked up and smiled. "Sounds good. I'll come to the kitchen with you—it's high time I got up and moved around a bit."

Mary fixed their tea and set out some shortbread cookies. She kept mulling the mystery while she sipped her fragrant blackberry tea.

"You're fidgeting." Betty eyed her over the rim of her cup. "What is it?"

Mary chuckled ruefully. "You caught me. It's half past eight, and I was wondering if that's too late to call Mr. Willoughby."

"I wouldn't think he'd go to bed this early."

"Thanks—I had just about decided to wait until I'm at the store tomorrow, but if you think it's all right, I'll call now."

She looked up the gallery owner's home number and placed the call. Mason Willoughby greeted her cordially.

"I'm sorry to bother you in the evening," Mary began.

"Don't worry about that," he said. "How may I assist you?"

"My sister and I have been doing a little digging into the family tree. You see, our great-uncle Lewis Nelson died recently, and we've begun to wonder about his wife, Maude. She died in 1950, but Betty and I have inherited several of her paintings. They're quite good, and—"

"You want to sell them?" Mr. Willoughby asked.

"Oh no. I'm sorry. That's not why I called." Mary hurried on, sensing she'd disappointed him. "You see, I found some old receipts in Uncle Lew's house. It seems Aunt Maude sold some of her work through the Ivy Bay Gallery in the late 1940s. We'd like to find out more, if that's possible."

"*Hmm.* Interesting. I didn't own the gallery back then, as I'm sure you know."

Mary chuckled. "I didn't think you were that old."

"Decidedly not. But I'll check into what records I have from previous owners and see if I can find out anything. What was the name again?"

"Maude Nelson. The paintings we have are signed that way, but her maiden name was Price, if that helps."

"Got it. And I'd love to have a peek at those canvases, if you and your sister are so inclined."

"That might be arranged," Mary said. "Right now, we don't want to sell them. One of them was supposed to go to a friend of my aunt's. The others were just sitting in Uncle Lew's attic. They're nice, colorful scenes of Provincetown in the mid-century, and they have an almost primitive look to them."

"You're making me drool." Mr. Willoughby laughed. "Give me a few days, and then come by the gallery. And in the meantime, if I find anything exciting, I'll call you."

"Perfect." Mary hung up. Betty had gone back to the living room and her book, taking her teacup with her. Mary told her what Mason had said and went up to the guest room. She wanted to take another look at the paintings.

As she studied the four hanging upstairs, she again felt the exuberance of the artist. She and Betty might want to keep them all—they were exactly the type of art Mary liked. They had a nostalgic feeling but not a dark, brooding sense of history. She loved recognizing some of the landmarks, though she couldn't help wishing some of them portrayed Ivy Bay.

The people Maude had depicted especially caught her attention. She was constantly noticing new things. In one of the street scenes, she noticed the tiny face of an infant in a baby carriage, and his mother's doting expression as she reached down to tuck the blanket in around him. In the harbor scene, a red-haired man wearing a slouch hat perched on a tumble of rocks that jutted out from shore, with a fishing pole in his hands and the line curving out into the calm water.

She sidestepped to stand in front of the community picnic scene and smiled. The gleeful children in the painting made her want to run and shout and clap her hands. Slowly, she let her eyes rove over the characters. This painting told a story. The tables laden with food, the bright quilts on the ground for picnickers to rest on, the vendors selling hot dogs and lemonade from their bunting-swathed booths, all brought joy and excitement to the tale.

Mary's gaze lingered on the figure of an old man, bent slightly over his cane, then slid on to another person behind him. She caught her breath, squinted at the painting for a moment, then stepped back in front of the harbor scene. She looked back and forth from one painting to the other. The red-haired man fishing in the harbor painting had also attended the picnic. In that one, he stood before a game booth, prepared to throw a dart at the target. His red hair peeked out from under his hat. She checked the other painting again. His face wasn't fully visible in either, but the two little figures looked like the same person. His build and attitude struck Mary as being alike, and in both, he wore the slouch hat and jeans, though his shirts were different.

She turned to another painting—the beach scene. In this one, people crowded the shore. A family built a sand castle, and several swimmers dotted the gentle waves. Sunbathers sprawled on their towels and blankets. A few colorful umbrellas shaded the fortunate. Mothers sat on the sand, watching their children frolic, and a child in the foreground crouched to pick a shell from the sand.

Then she found him. The red-haired man was also at the beach. Again he wore the jeans and the floppy hat, with a white T-shirt shaded to almost blend with the sand. He was far down the beach, his back to the viewer, with a dog trotting beside him. Just a hint of his red hair showed beneath the brim of the hat, but Mary was sure it was him.

He was easier to find in the fourth painting, the one with the church. He leaned on a fence, seemingly conversing with another man. His face showed more in this one, but even so, he was turned toward his companion and the figures were small compared to those in the foreground.

Mary noted the man's location in each painting. He took part in a different activity in each one. She wondered if he was also in the painting down in the sunroom—the one with the letter to Elle.

She strode to her room and got the photos she'd printed out of the five paintings and then went downstairs. Without disturbing Betty, she hurried into the sunroom and switched on the light.

Now that she knew what to look for, he was easy to spot. In this view of Provincetown's main street, the red-haired man was entering a shop—a grocery, by the look of it, situated next door to an art gallery. The market's window held a display of colorful produce. Maybe she could identify the actual location.

Time to get Betty's input. Mary took the photos out to the living room and paused by her sister's chair.

Betty looked up. "Hi! What do you have there?"

"My pictures of Maude's paintings. I want to show you something."

"Oh?" Betty raised the back of her chair and laid her book on the end table.

"This is the first painting—the one for Elle." Mary held out that photograph first, as the man was larger and easier to see in that one, and his red hair showed plainly. "Do you see this man here, going into the market?"

Betty peered at the photograph. "Yes. What about him?"

Mary handed her the next picture. "He's also in this painting. See him there, by the fence?"

Betty frowned and brought the picture a little closer to her face. "You think it's the same man? The hat does look the same."

"I do," Mary said. "Notice the red hair, hat, and jeans. This man is in every one of the paintings."

"You're joking."

"I'm not."

Betty looked up at her, wrinkles lining her forehead. "Why didn't we notice that before?"

Mary shrugged. "All the paintings are really busy, with dozens of people in them. I notice new things every time I look at them. And tonight, I noticed this man." She held out the harbor scene. "He's far away in this one, but you can still see the red hair." She pointed to the fisherman on the distant pile of rocks.

"Oh my," Betty said softly. She reached for the next one.

Mary let her study the picnic scene on her own until she tapped it.

"He's throwing darts."

"That's right."

She handed Betty the last photograph, the one of the crowded beach.

"Oh dear, there must be a hundred people in this one. Why don't you just show me?"

Mary leaned over and pointed to the man walking down the beach with the dog.

"An Irish setter," Betty said.

"Probably. You can't see the man's face, but he's wearing the jeans and the hat. In the painting, you can even see a tiny bit of red hair on the back of his neck. It doesn't show up well in this photo though."

Betty stacked the pictures and handed them back to her. "What does it mean?"

"I'm not sure. And there may be other people in more than one painting—I haven't had time to check yet. But this guy...he has to be someone Maude knew."

"You don't think it's Uncle Lew, do you?"

Mary shook her head. "Not really. I mean, he didn't have red hair."

"No, in all the old photos it was brown before he went gray."

"Right. And nobody in the Nelson family has red hair."

"No one I can think of," Betty admitted. "So this man is important."

"He might be." Mary sat down on the couch and leafed slowly through the pictures again. "Maybe we can find out who he was."

"The dog," Betty said.

"That's a good clue. But the dog is only in one painting—I think. I'll look for it again in the others. The man always seems to be lounging around—fishing, playing a game, talking to someone." She gazed down at the church scene. "This seems to be the only one where he's engaging with another person. In the beach one, he's walking alone, except for the dog. And in this street scene, he's going into a store, but he seems to be alone."

"*Hmm.*" Betty smiled and shook her head. "Not a lot to go on, but you might find some older people in Provincetown who could tell you who he was."

"It's hard to tell his age." Mary looked up. "He could still be alive."

"He'd be really old."

"Yes. But Uncle Lew lived this long. He was ninety-two, but…well, I'm just saying."

"It's possible." Betty leaned back and gazed up toward the ceiling. "Do you think Aunt Maude really drowned?"

"I don't know." Mary laid the photos on the coffee table. "We have a couple of people in Provincetown saying they remembered that, but I'm thinking they could be confusing the reports of a drowning in Ivy Bay with her death. Chief McArthur's going to try to find the autopsy report on that body for me."

"But you said the funeral home never had her body." Betty's blue eyes clouded. "Wouldn't that be consistent with her drowning? What if two people drowned that year, and Aunt Maude's body was never recovered?"

"I guess it's possible," Mary said, "but highly coincidental."

"Why else would Uncle Lew have held the funeral? I can't think of many ways a person would die and not leave a body behind."

Mary nodded slowly, working things out in her mind. She liked it when clues came neatly together. This mystery was too messy for her liking.

"The way I see it, there are several possibilities. Number one, and I haven't ruled this out, is that Maude died of natural causes."

"That's what we always thought."

"Yes, but that theory's not looking good right now." Mary frowned, hating to unsettle Betty. "I think we have to consider other options. If we want to know the truth, I mean, and all of this has me really curious."

"What are you thinking? Besides the drowning, I mean?" Betty leaned toward her and watched Mary earnestly.

"Second," Mary said cautiously, "I've wondered if she ran off with another man—as the letter suggested—and faked her own death so she could disappear without being looked for. She did tell her longtime friend she was running away."

Betty sank back in the recliner, clearly not satisfied with this explanation. "That would take a lot of work."

Mary nodded. "It seems really far-fetched that she would do that, but I'm just saying it's a possibility."

"Aunt Maude was an artist."

"Yes. What are you thinking?"

Betty shrugged. "It sounds a little silly, but do you think it could have been a publicity stunt?"

Mary had never considered that path. "*Hmm.* Seems unlikely. She wasn't in that league, was she? Her paintings were nice, but she wasn't exactly famous."

"Maybe she wanted to be." Betty smiled sheepishly. "I'm just trying to feed that active imagination of yours."

"You're doing a good job." Mary laughed. "Okay, let's think about that. It doesn't seem to me that she had very many paintings out there, and she left several in the house when she disappeared. If she hoped they'd increase in value, why didn't she put those in galleries before she left? I'd think she'd have offered them for sale before the stunt, if it was one. Then buyers could come forward and fight over them."

"I suppose that makes sense," Betty said. "And as far as we know, Uncle Lew never put them on the market. It seemed more like he wanted to forget about them."

"Ready for my third theory?" Mary asked.

"Sure. Go ahead."

"What if she left Uncle Lew, but she died soon afterward?"

"*Hmm.* I see that fitting some of the facts. But how did she die, if not the drowning thing? And if she left Uncle Lew for another man, why did *he* hold the funeral, not the mystery man she ran off with?"

"Good question. For the family, I suppose." Mary picked up the photographs and stared down at the red-haired man in the street scene. "Wouldn't it be wild if this man was the mystery man?"

"Aunt Maude's…champion?" Betty asked so hesitantly that Mary smiled.

"I just had a thought. What if he was at the funeral?"

"Oh!" Betty's blue eyes widened. "Of course. If he loved her, he would be, wouldn't he? Why, his name could be in the guest book!"

"I'll go through them and see if I can identify all the guests' names. It will take a while, but it might be worth it."

"I think that's a promising lead."

Mary laid the photos on the table and sighed. "But it may not pan out." After a moment, she smiled over at Betty. "I didn't realize when we went to see that lawyer about our inheritance that it would lead to so many questions. At first, I just wanted to know what had happened to Aunt Maude. Now there's so much more."

"I'm with you," Betty said. "These paintings have made me wonder too—especially about that redheaded man."

EIGHT

◆◆◆

As she dressed for her prayer group meeting on Tuesday morning, Mary continued to think about the possibilities. Was it credible that her great-aunt had left Uncle Lew and died shortly afterward? Did her decision to leave the marriage contribute to her death? Mary didn't like that idea, but she couldn't rule it out.

At the time Maude wrote the letter to Elle, Uncle Lew had apparently been angry with her to the point of harming her. Maude had made plans to run off with another man. But what if that didn't work out? What if she had a mishap in trying to get away and drowned, or otherwise met a tragic death? Even if Maude had died in some other way, Mary told herself, people might have linked it with the drowning as their memories faded.

But the question remained: Was Aunt Maude's death natural, an accident, or murder? Though Mary doubted it could have been murder without folks remembering a public outcry, nothing seemed to make complete sense.

Over the breakfast table, she laid her latest speculations before Betty.

"If Elle is still alive, she may know something. Remember how Aunt Maude said in the letter that she might contact Elle later?"

"Yes. But we have no evidence that any of her friends or family ever heard from her again." Betty refilled their coffee cups and poured milk into hers, then passed the pitcher to Mary.

"We have to look beyond the obvious." Mary took a bite of her toast and thought as she chewed it slowly. "We need to find out what role Elle played in Maude's disappearance."

"If any." Betty eyed her pointedly. "Elle never got the painting. If Maude contacted her later on, don't you think she'd have asked about that, and told Elle she left it for her?"

"Maybe Uncle Lew wouldn't give it to her." Mary frowned, unwilling to give up what she still considered a promising lead. "Or if Maude did tell Elle about it, maybe they agreed to forget about it because they didn't want Uncle Lew to know where she was—or even that Maude was still alive."

"Back to the faked-death theory?"

"Or the hiding-from-the-violent-husband theory."

"I hate that one." Betty took a swallow of her coffee.

"I hate this whole thing," Mary said. Though the puzzle intrigued her, the unhappiness of the people involved disturbed her. "I don't want Uncle Lew to be a mean man or a criminal. I don't even want him and Aunt Maude to be at odds."

"Mar, it was more than sixty years ago, and we can't change that part," Betty said gently, setting her cup down on the saucer.

"I know. And I realize it may be painful, but I need to know the truth about them." She sighed. "I'm sure whatever those two did, they thought they were doing the right thing. Maude when she decided to leave Lew, and Lew when he planned that memorial service—all of it. Like it says in Proverbs, 'Every way of a man is right in his own eyes, but the Lord weigheth the hearts.' I just wish we knew their hearts."

"That's something we'll probably never really uncover," Betty said.

"Oh, I know. I'm just too much of an idealist." Mary rose and rinsed their dishes and put them in the dishwasher. She wanted this riddle to be answered and tied up neatly, the way the mysteries always were in the novels she loved. The criminals were always caught in those stories, and mysterious deaths were always explained.

A few minutes later, she drove to the church for her prayer meeting, knowing Rebecca would open the bookshop if she didn't get there by ten. Before going inside, she texted Rebecca, reminding her that today was the day for her prayer group, but her mind was still on the unhappy couple as she entered the church.

Mary was glad to see her faithful friends, and each one brought requests for the group to pray about. After the meeting, Dorothy Johnson touched Mary's arm and held her back as the others went out the door. This morning, Dorothy had a spark in her eyes.

"Mary!" Her voice was low and conspiratorial. "We want to have a baby shower for Brooke. Would you serve on the committee?"

"Oh well...what would I have to do?"

"We'll get together two or three times to plan it. We're thinking of having a tea and art party."

Mary smiled. "That goes along with the theme of her painting classes."

"Exactly. Will you?"

Dorothy looked so sincere and so hopeful that Mary couldn't say no. Sometimes Dorothy could get a little controlling, not to say bossy, but she and Mary got along quite well nowadays.

"All right, I will. When's the first meeting?"

"Tomorrow night at my house. Can you come at seven?"

Mary squeezed Dorothy's arm. "I'll be there."

Mary focused her curiosity on Elle Wetherly. At the town office on Wednesday afternoon, she learned the location of the Wetherly family's old house. But Elle's parents had sold it and moved out of Ivy Bay about ten years after Maude disappeared. Though she called on Irene Billings again and phoned two other elderly residents, Mary couldn't get a line on Elle's adult life. The best she could do was one woman's recollection that Elle had gone away to college and hadn't lived long with her parents afterward.

She squeezed in a quick trip to the newspaper offices later in the afternoon and spent an hour combing the archives. Nothing about Elle turned up in the 1950s, but finally she found a wedding announcement from the year 1960. Mary studied it, surprised Elle had married so late. She must have been well into her thirties.

She called Rebecca, since it was half past five, and asked her to close the store. Mary didn't want to rush dinner in order to get to Dorothy's house on time.

When she got home, she told Betty about the wedding announcement she had found.

"If she and Aunt Maude were the same age, she didn't get married until she was thirty-seven." Mary shook her head. "And she was so pretty."

"Maybe that was a second marriage." Betty calmly went on tossing the salad for their supper.

"You could be right. Still, the announcement gave her name before the wedding as Wetherly. Some divorced women do go back to their maiden names though." Mary opened the silverware drawer and took out the cutlery they would need. "It probably doesn't matter. What may help is that I found her husband's name. She married a man named Harold Weir, and guess what Elle was doing at the time?"

"Doing? You mean for a job?" Betty shrugged.

"She was a professor of literature at a college in Connecticut." When she named the college, Betty's eyebrows shot up.

"That's a classy private institution. Known for excellence in academics."

"Maybe that's why she married so late," Mary said.

"Wasn't she the wild one in high school? I hadn't thought she was all that scholarly."

"Irene said she was always up to something, but that doesn't mean she wasn't a good student. She was supposedly very intelligent. Of course, Irene thought she'd married young too."

"How old was Aunt Maude when she married Uncle Lew?"

"Twenty. And Elle still used the Wetherly name then, so I don't think she was married yet."

Betty set the salad bowl on the table and took her seat. "Maybe Irene remembered wrong. Elle could have gotten a job someplace else and moved away. If Irene wasn't close to her, she might have assumed in retrospect that Elle got married in that period."

———

Mary left Gus with Betty that evening while she drove to Dorothy's house for the committee meeting. Dorothy greeted her at the door of the historic old house and led her to the living room, where the pastor's wife, Tricia Miles, was chatting with Jill Sanderson and Bernice Foster, two other women who belonged to Mary's prayer group.

"I think we're all here." Dorothy waved Mary to a seat on the sofa beside Bernice and walked to a rocking chair Mary suspected was her favorite. "Thank you all so much for coming. Now, I have a few ideas for the baby shower. I know we all want to make Brooke feel special. She's done so much for the church nursery program, and we all appreciate her hard work."

Mary smiled and listened, knowing it would take Dorothy a few minutes to make her presentation. She couldn't be rushed, but she was a very good organizer. With her in charge, the shower couldn't be a flop.

"We all know Brooke is an artist," Dorothy went on. "She's offering painting classes called Tea, Paint, and Sympathy."

"Aren't you taking that class, Mary?" Tricia asked, smiling at her across the room.

"Yes, Betty and I are both enrolled, and we're enjoying it very much."

Dorothy nodded. "I thought we might carry the art theme through for the baby shower."

"That sounds cool," Jill said. "We can make artsy decorations—palettes and brushes, things like that."

"Well, yes." Dorothy cleared her throat. "That does go along with what I was thinking. And for the gifts, Brooke's mother tells me she has registered at a couple of stores, but I thought we could also ask each person to bring an art supply for the child."

Bernice sat up and blinked at her. "Art supplies for a baby?"

"Oh, I realize the child couldn't use them right away, but I thought it would be fun—you know, whimsical. And Brooke could put them aside for later. Finger paints, crayons, that sort of thing."

"It's not a bad idea," Mary said. "We could use things like paintbrushes for package ornaments."

"Sure," Tricia said. "It'll be cute. And three or four years down the road, Brooke will have supplies ready to use as needed."

Mary's mind whirled. Could she track down a little beret made to fit a baby? Already she wanted to find something unusual but not totally impractical. Maybe a little smock dress, since Brooke was sure the baby was a girl.

She smiled at Dorothy. "I think it would be a cute theme. It's perfect for Brooke, and the art items will be good conversation starters."

At the end of an hour's discussion, the plans for the shower were well under way. They set a date for their next meeting and enjoyed tea and cookies together before leaving. Mary had scribbled notes about her assignments for the shower preparations, but her rebellious mind soon veered back to the mystery.

Now that she had Elle Wetherly's married name, she ought to be able to get a line on the woman and find out where she had gone. The newspaper announcement had described her husband as "Harold Weir, Hartford, Conn." That, coupled with the fact that Elle had been teaching at a private college in Connecticut, prompted Mary to start a deeper computer search that evening when she got home, focusing on Weirs in the neighboring state.

Mary followed many paths that turned out to be dead ends. She found an Edward Weir who fabricated sculptures from old junk, and an Elizabeth Weir who had won a Mother of the Year contest in a suburban town the previous year. A pastor named George Weir served a church in Waterbury. There seemed to be many interesting people named Weir living in Connecticut. Mary was almost ready to call it quits for the evening when she turned up a scholarly article on the author Willa Cather, written by professor Elle W. Weir.

Mary read it avidly. She had read *O Pioneers!* and *My Antonia* many years ago, and she found Elle's analysis of the author's style fascinating. She checked the note at the end of the article. It was written almost thirty years ago, and Elle was still teaching at the small private college when she wrote it.

Mary started a new search, specifying the town where the college was located. To her surprise, she turned up a listing and a phone number for an E. W. Weir currently living in the college town. Was it possible Elle had worked there until retirement and then stayed nearby?

Mary printed out the information and hurried to the kitchen.

"Betty! Guess what!"

Betty was taking a package of chicken from the freezer. She opened the door to the refrigerator and put it in, then shut the door.

"I can't imagine what you're up to now." She turned to face Mary with a smile. "Just tell me."

"I think I found Elle." Mary showed her the paper she'd printed. "It has to be her."

"I've done too much genealogy research to jump to that conclusion," Betty said. "It might be her, but it could also be a relative, or a coincidence—someone else with the same initials."

"Oh, come on! You think it's her, don't you? I can't believe you're that pessimistic. My own sister!"

Betty laughed. "Why don't you call and find out?"

"Maybe I will."

"I'll be right here to support you."

"What? You think I'll faint if it's really her?" Mary chuckled. "All right, I'll do it." She took the cordless phone and punched in the number. She sat down on a stool near the white tile counter and waited while the call processed and the phone on the other end began to ring.

Betty opened a cupboard and took out one of her favorite cookbooks.

"Hello?" said a voice in Mary's ear.

Mary jumped. "Oh, hello. My name is Mary Fisher." She pulled in a breath, telling herself to calm down. "I-I'm looking for someone named Elle Wetherly Weir. Could I possibly have found the right person?"

"Well, that's my name. May I ask what your interest is?"

"Of course." Mary hauled in a deep breath. "I had a great-aunt who died in 1950. I never knew her personally, but I'm interested in her as part of my family heritage. I recently inherited some paintings that she did, and I'd like to know more about her as an artist too. Her name was Maude Price Nelson."

Mary stopped talking. The silence was so profound that she feared for a moment that she had lost the connection.

"Maude," the woman said at last. "You're related to Maude."

"Yes." Mary bit her lip and waited.

"I hardly know what to say."

"You did know her, then? I found pictures of you in her school yearbook. I'm told you were Aunt Maude's best friend."

"We were very close." Her voice sounded thicker, more emotional.

"I know she cared a great deal about you." Mary looked over at her sister. Betty still stood before the cupboard, cradling the cookbook in her arms and watching her anxiously.

"That's odd," Mrs. Weir said, "because she never contacted me after...after a certain incident. At first, I thought she was dead, but later...I assumed she was angry with me all this time. I have wondered though...what became of her."

"So do I." Mary gazed at Betty as she spoke. "My sister and I would like very much to talk with you. Would it be possible for us to come visit you? We live in Ivy Bay."

"Ivy Bay." Mrs. Weir chuckled. "It's been a long time since I've been there, or talked to anyone from there. What was your name again?"

"Mary Fisher, but I was a Nelson. My father was Davis Nelson."

"Oh yes, sure. I knew Davis and Esther."

"Did you?" Mary smiled for the first time. "They're both gone now, and my sister and I are heirs to Uncle Lew's estate. That's how we found Aunt Maude's paintings."

"So Lew is dead too."

Her voice had gone flat, and Mary hesitated.

"Yes. He died a few weeks ago."

Betty came over to stand beside her. "Tell her."

Mary looked up and whispered, "You mean...?"

"The painting for her."

"We found five paintings," Mary said into the phone. "One of them...had a note attached. It says 'To Elle.' We've been looking for you, in hopes we could find you and deliver it to you."

"What? One of Maude's paintings? For me?"

"We think she intended for you to have it when she left Uncle Lew in 1950," Mary said. "But we also found the guest book from her funeral. We're still sorting out the details of what happened. May we come talk to you?"

"Yes," Elle said. "Please—as soon as possible."

NINE

◆◆

Saturday was the first day both Mary and Betty could get away. Elle's home was a two-hour drive to the southwest, and Mary took her car. Well wrapped in the trunk was Elle's painting, and Maude's letter was tucked safely in Mary's purse.

The college town held a quaint charm, even in early February. They rolled past the stone-and-brick buildings of the campus, shrouded in snow. All was quiet except for a few students strolling the cleared walkways. The GPS guided them beyond the dormitories and classroom buildings to a quiet neighborhood of small but expensive-looking homes.

"There it is," Betty said. "Number 165."

Mary pulled into the driveway and shut off the engine. They sat for a moment looking at the elegant little cottage. Its stone facade curved gracefully up to the cedar-shingled roof. The front door and windows formed Gothic arches, and granite steps led up to a small covered porch.

"It's a fairy-tale cottage," Mary said.

She got out and took the painting from the trunk. As she and Betty walked up to the porch, a gray-haired woman opened the door. Mary searched her face for the girl whose pictures she had studied in the yearbook. Though her skin looked papery and fragile, the delicate bone structure and large, eager eyes still gave her an elfin air.

"I'm Mary, and this is my sister, Betty Emerson."

"And I'm Elle. Come in."

She stepped aside, and a large gray-and-white speckled Rottweiler behind her eyed them ominously. Mary froze and swallowed hard.

"Tad, go lie down," Elle said firmly.

The dog obediently turned and slunk through a doorway.

"You'll have to excuse him. That's his job—intimidating people."

"No problem," Mary said.

"I got him when my husband died. I don't like living alone."

They entered directly into the living room. Two walls were covered almost entirely with bookshelves. Over an antique writing desk hung a seascape that might have been Ivy Bay, but it was definitely not Maude's style.

Mary held the wrapped painting she carried toward Elle. "This is the picture Aunt Maude wanted you to have."

Elle's hands trembled as she reached for the fabric-wrapped frame. "I can't tell you what this means to me."

"Let me help you." Mary set the frame down so it leaned against the old cobbler's bench that served as a coffee table.

"Forgive me," Elle said. "I should have taken your coats first thing. I'm a little excited, I guess."

"That's all right," Betty said, removing her loden coat. "We can lay them right here on this chair."

"Oh no, there's a closet." Elle gestured toward the far wall.

"Let me." Betty waited for Mary to take off her jacket, and she took both of their coats to the door Elle had indicated.

"Would you like to open this now?" Mary asked. "Perhaps on a table?"

"Yes. The kitchen, I think."

Elle led the way, and Mary followed with the painting. Betty came in a moment later as Mary laid the painting on the round kitchen table and peeled back the clean white sheet she had wrapped around it instead of the dusty old one Uncle Lew had used.

Elle caught her breath and stood unmoving for a minute, gazing down at the painting. Mary watched her face. The old woman's eyes moved here and there, taking in the many elements of the scene, caressing the work of her long-gone friend.

"It's so like her." Her voice cracked.

"We love it," Mary said.

Betty stirred. "We're delighted that we could bring it to you."

"Thank you." Tears filled Elle's eyes, and she blinked rapidly. "I was so hurt, thinking she didn't care about me."

"Oh, but she did, very much." Mary glanced at Betty, and her sister nodded. "There's more, Mrs. Weir."

"What do you mean?"

"Elle left you a letter. We found it inside the paper backing on the painting." Mary opened her purse and took out the folded paper. "Perhaps you'd like to sit down and read it."

"Yes. Thank you." Elle pulled out a chair and plopped into it.

Mary handed her the letter. "Forgive us for reading it— but we might not have found you if we hadn't done so."

Elle's hand trembled as she took it. "I...I should offer you tea or something."

Betty stepped around the table. "That's not necessary, but if you'd like a cup, I'd be happy to fix it while you read the letter."

Elle wiped a tear from the corner of her eye. "That would be nice. The kettle is there, on the stove, and I set out cups and..." She let it trail off and turned her attention to the paper in her hands.

Betty walked to the counter and quietly began to fill the teakettle, but Mary sat near Elle and waited while the old woman unfolded the letter and peered down at it.

After a moment, Elle's tears spilled over. This time, she made no effort to stop them. "Well."

Mary nodded but said nothing.

Elle glanced up at her. "It seems obvious Maude was determined to get away quickly when she wrote that, without seeing Lew again."

"We thought so too," Mary said. "She hid the letter in the painting she'd labeled for you, hoping you'd find it but that Uncle Lew wouldn't see it."

Elle sighed. "She didn't want him to have another chance to hurt her."

Mary cleared her throat. "Do you know if he had hurt her before?"

"I don't think so—not physically. But she suffered greatly from things he said."

"The note seemed to indicate that this might have been the first time he...he struck her."

"Yes. 'Lew went too far this time.' That sort of implies he hadn't before." Elle's mouth twitched. "He wore her down, you know."

"No, we didn't know. My parents never gave us a hint of anything like that. All we knew was that Aunt Maude died in 1950—the year I was born—and that she was an artist. That was about it. We always assumed she died of an accident or of disease. Do you know anything about that?"

Elle shook her head. "After she disappeared, there was a funeral. It was weeks afterward though." She fingered the edge of the wooden frame. "I'm so glad she wanted me to have one of her paintings. And it's so cheerful and sunny."

"Yes, they all are," Mary said. "Her style is almost whimsical."

"Joyful." Elle smiled as she gazed down at the little figures in the village scene.

The teakettle whistled, and Betty bustled about, filling the cups on the counter. Mary wondered if she could tactfully find out how much Elle knew—more than she had revealed so far, Mary was certain. Had she urged Maude to leave her husband, and Uncle Lew suspected as much? That might explain why he had never given Elle the painting. In her letter, Maude had confided to her friend about the argument and her general plans to leave.

Gently, she asked, "Did you see Maude after her fight with Lew—the one where he struck her?"

"Never. She dropped out of sight, and I suspected she had left him."

"Why did you think that?" Mary asked.

"She'd talked about it before. The possibility, I mean. She was very unhappy."

"But—where would she go? She didn't go back to her parents' home, did she? We'd have known, at least if she'd stayed with them long."

Betty brought the cups over and then the cream and sugar. She sat down opposite Mary, and they all settled in with their tea.

After Elle had stirred a spoonful of sugar into hers, she looked up at Mary. "It was so long ago I suppose it doesn't matter now. You girls—well, I don't suppose you'll see it the way it was then. Quite a scandal, you know, for a woman to leave her husband."

"I can imagine," Betty said. "We appreciate any information you can share with us."

Elle sipped her tea and set the cup down. "All right, I'll say it right out. Maude had been seeing another man."

"We wondered, because of what she said in the note," Mary said.

Betty nodded. "The one person she could trust."

Elle's lips skewed. "Yes. She felt she couldn't trust me at the time, though she did leave this behind for me. I wish I'd known. Oh, how I wish I'd known. I surely would have helped her, you know."

"I'm so sorry you had no inkling all these years," Mary said.

Elle inhaled deeply. "Well, what's past is past. Lew probably kept the painting out of spite. He had quite a temper, but I suppose you know that."

"We never saw it," Betty said. "We only saw him occasionally, at holidays and on family visits. Mary and I used to spend summers in Ivy Bay with our grandparents, and sometimes Uncle Lew would come to their house, but he lived in Provincetown, and we really didn't see him much. I've lived in Ivy Bay all my adult life, but even so, I didn't see him more than a couple of times a year."

"He may have mellowed over time," Mary suggested.

"I guess anything's possible."

"What happened to her?" Mary asked. "And how did you even learn about her being gone, since you didn't get her letter?"

"I tried to call her, and no one answered. I drove to their house, and no one was there. The next-door neighbor told me Maude was gone. Said she'd up and left her husband. It was such a surprise, and not a good one."

"What did you do?" Betty asked.

"I went over to Lew's office, but he didn't want to talk to me. He accused me of egging her on to leave him. He was pretty nasty about it, I'll tell you. I started to protest, but a client of his came in, so I left. But at that point, I did think she'd run off with this other man. There was no question of her dying. I was really shocked when I heard that bit of news."

"You didn't attend the funeral," Mary said.

"Well, yes and no."

"Your name wasn't in the guest book."

Elle took a swallow of her tea and then scowled. "I went to the funeral home that day, hoping to find out what had happened to Maude. But Lew saw me in the foyer, when I first went in. I hadn't even gotten through the line to sign the guest book when he lit into me."

"At the funeral parlor?" Betty stared at her.

"That's right. He was pretty riled. Said that I'd done enough. His face was all red, and he was getting loud. He said I wasn't welcome, and I might as well leave. So I did. I wasn't sure what he meant—probably still thinking I'd encouraged Maude to leave him. Anyway, I left without signing the guest book. I was humiliated and angry at Lew. Later, I got the scoop from another friend. She said Maude had drowned, and her body had washed ashore, but later—"

"Yes?" Mary said. "Later, what?"

Elle shrugged. "The official report came out later, saying the body they found wasn't her. It was so long ago…but I remember it made me wonder why Lew was so eager to bury her…or at least, to hold a funeral."

"I spoke to the funeral director," Mary said. "Well, to his son. They have the old records, and he told me there was no body for Maude's memorial service. They thought she had drowned. At least that's what Lew told them. The family wanted a service for closure, even though they hadn't found her body."

Elle shook her head. "That doesn't make sense to me. Does it to you?"

"Not really."

"Not to me either," Betty said. "I do a lot of family history, and I never saw a precise death date for Maude. The date of that memorial service is all we have to go on."

Elle sat in silence for several seconds and then looked around suddenly. "Oh, I had a loaf of banana bread. It's over there, in the plastic container."

"I'll get it." Betty stood and went to the counter.

Mary accepted a slice out of courtesy and was glad she did. The sweet bread was very moist and tasty.

"This is delicious," she said.

"Yes." Betty smiled at Elle. "You have a great recipe."

"Thank you. I got it from Maude, not long after she married."

"Really?" Betty asked, clearly delighted. "Would you mind sharing it with us?"

"I'd be glad to." Elle finished her slice and wiped her fingers on a napkin. "It's right here, in my recipe box." She rose and got the recipe for Betty, along with a pen and a blank card.

"I'd be happy to copy it," Betty said.

"All right." Elle sat down again and turned her attention to Mary. "You know, Maude's disappearance was a shock to me, even though I knew she was unhappy in her marriage and wanted to leave it. I never thought she'd carry through. Or if she did, I supposed she'd tell me her plans."

"So you knew nothing about where she went?" Betty asked, her eyes wide in sympathy.

"Not a thing."

"Then I guess you couldn't have helped her escape," Mary said, a bit disappointed. "That was one of my theories. I admit I hoped you could point us to a clue about Maude's destination when she left Provincetown."

"I'm sorry I can't," Elle said. "In fact, I tried to talk her out of leaving Lew. I guess that was a mistake."

"How so?" Betty asked.

Elle's lip quivered. "When I first learned about the affair, I urged Maude to end it and make up with Lew. I was sure she'd regret it if she didn't, and that staying in the marriage was best for her. We had a big fight about it. Maude was near her breaking point then, I guess—nearer than I knew. I...thought I knew what was best, but that was rather arrogant of me. After all, I'd never been married, or had to live constantly with an angry person."

"We can never completely understand what another person is going through," Mary said. "I'm sure you only wanted to help."

"I truly did. But she wouldn't listen to me. Then I made my biggest mistake." Elle's voice wavered. "I threatened to tell Lew that she was seeing another man, hoping that would shock Maude into breaking off her relationship. She begged me not to, and I felt terrible. I never told Lew anything."

"But he found out anyway," Mary said. "He hit her."

"I'm not sure if he knew about the other man or not. I never knew that Lew harmed her physically—until today. I wondered, but I had no proof. I'd heard them argue before, and Maude told me about times when he got angry and ranted at her. But I was never sure he'd taken it further until I saw this letter written in her own hand." Elle gazed bleakly down at the paper. "I really didn't think she'd go."

"But you said she had talked about it." Mary studied the woman's face.

Elle nodded. "She had, but even so, when she disappeared, it seemed very sudden. And I was hurt that she hadn't told me. Now...now I know she tried. I thought the reason I didn't hear from her was because Maude was still angry with me, because I had said I'd tell Lew. I worried about it—that I had forced her hand. I thought she was so mad that she deliberately left me wondering." She looked up, her face drawn in pain. "And then I heard she had died."

"You heard she had drowned," Mary said.

"Yes, but as I said, later I wondered if that was true." Elle gave a mirthless laugh and shook her head. "I even wondered if she'd staged it, to keep Lew from following her. But time went on, and no one heard from her. I visited the cemetery in Provincetown before I moved away, and I saw her gravestone. Tell me—was it real?"

"We believed it was," Betty said.

"But we have no proof either," Mary added. "I've been trying to get conclusive evidence myself—proof that Aunt Maude really died, and what the circumstances were. All this time, I've been trying to find out how she really died. Maybe I was asking the wrong questions."

"If she didn't..." Elle looked from Mary to Betty. "If she were still alive, why didn't she contact me after she left and tell me she was all right?"

Mary had puzzled over the same question. The letter suggested Maude wanted her friend to know she was safe. And yet she had never followed up on it.

"Maybe she still thought I'd tell Lew if I knew where she was. Pretty funny, when Lew was sure I'd had something to do with her going away." Elle picked up her teacup, looked into it for a moment, and set it down.

"Let me fix you some more." Betty rose.

"Thank you. Nice and strong, please."

"Whether she died soon after or not," Mary said, while Betty heated more water, "this incident when Lew hit her seems to have been the turning point, the moment that spurred her to action."

Elle nodded.

"This man she planned to meet that night," Mary said, watching her carefully, "do you know who he was?"

"I wish I did, but she never told me. Even though we were good friends, she protected herself in that way. I wish more than anything I knew who he was and where they went."

TEN

——◆◆◆——

Mary sipped her second cup of tea, mulling over what Elle had told them. Instead of answers, she now had more questions. She believed Elle had been a true friend to Aunt Maude and had advised her to do what she felt was right—to stay true to her husband. Perhaps Elle would have acted differently if she had known Lew would turn to violence, but there was no way they could ever know that now.

Of one thing, Mary had no doubt—Elle had absorbed a great deal of pain when her best friend had disappeared without contacting her. How strongly did Elle's actions, and her threat to tell Lew about the affair, figure into Maude's disappearance? Would she have snuck off if Elle had offered a more sympathetic ear?

Elle had acted as her own conscience led her at the time, and Mary could see no benefit of adding to her feelings of guilt. But she still might be able to help them learn what had happened to Aunt Maude.

Mary set down her teacup and smiled ruefully. "Would you mind if I asked you something a little off-the-wall?"

"Like what?" Elle asked.

"Betty and I heard all sorts of rumors from people who lived near the Nelsons in Provincetown, and from older people in Ivy Bay who knew them. I wondered what you thought, deep down. Was Lew Nelson responsible for Maude's death?"

Elle let out a long, slow breath. "Doubtful. Not directly, anyway. I do recall that people were suspicious, especially when he held the funeral for Maude."

For a fleeting moment, Mary wondered if Elle knew more than she was letting on. What if Maude *did* communicate with Elle after she left Ivy Bay, but swore her friend to secrecy? Was Elle still covering her friend's tracks?

"I think she did run away with that fellow," Elle said. "But where she went, I have no idea, or even if she's still alive."

"She never told you who it was." Mary knew Elle had stated as much, but she wanted to be sure.

"No. I wondered if he was married, or if he was someone I knew and she wanted to be sure I couldn't possibly reveal his name to Lew. I honestly hoped I could convince her to break it off, but it seems my efforts backfired. When she did leave, I thought she didn't trust me enough to leave me a clue. But Lew seemed to think I knew all about it anyway." Elle closed her eyes for a moment, then opened them and looked into Mary's face. "Do you suppose he threw me out of the funeral home so I wouldn't tell anyone she wasn't really dead? Maybe he thought I knew where she was and would expose his little sham."

Mary looked over at Betty, who shrugged helplessly.

"That's an interesting idea," Mary said.

Elle sighed. "I wish I'd been a better friend to her. Maybe then I'd have realized Maude was in danger."

Mary still found it hard to think of Uncle Lew as a violent villain, but what else could she think? In Maude's letter, she had stated that he hit her and that was her reason for leaving.

But had she really left Provincetown that night? Did she really die back in 1950? And if so, how? The thought that Uncle Lew could have killed her made Mary squirm. But what of the mysterious man with whom Maude was involved? Maybe he wasn't ready to run off with Maude. Did they quarrel about it? Maybe he was married, as Elle had suggested, and never really intended to have a future with Maude. But she suddenly told him she was ready. Had he decided to change her plans for her?

There had to be some other explanation. If only Mary knew for sure whether or not Aunt Maude had died that night...or even that year. So far she hadn't found an official death record for Maude, though she had searched online for any records of Maude Price Nelson's death. That should have been a red flag, she realized now. She determined to change the focus of her investigation from the manner of Aunt Maude's death to the timing.

Up until now, the police hadn't been much help. She hoped Chief McArthur would come up with something soon. But until that happened, she had to follow whatever leads she could find. Right now it seemed that unless they could identify and locate the man Maude had been in love with, Mary had little chance of unraveling the tangled story.

"There's one thing I wanted to ask you about in the painting." Mary rose and went to stand beside Elle. "Do you see this man right here?" She pointed to the red-haired man entering the market on the village street.

"Yes, I see him." Elle gazed down at the canvas.

"Is he anyone you know? I ask, because he's in all the paintings we found."

"Really!" Elle bent closer. "*Hmm.* You can't really see his face."

Mary sighed. "No, and it's not clear in any of them. I hoped you might recognize him."

"I'll think on it," Elle said slowly, "but nothing's jumping out at me."

Betty rose and walked around the table. She touched Elle's shoulder gently. "Mrs. Weir—Elle—you were a good friend to Maude. You saw her acting recklessly, and you tried to guide her into a better path. Don't blame yourself for what happened—no matter what became of her. It isn't your fault."

Mary's eyes filled with tears. "I agree," she said softly. "Thank you for what you tried to do. And I assure you, I won't stop looking into this."

"Thank you." Elle's voice quivered. "We may never know what happened. I resigned myself to that a long time ago. But if you do find out something, please let me know."

"I will," Mary said.

Elle pushed back her chair. "I have some old letters and notes that I saved, from when we were young. I doubt it will help you, but you might see something there that I didn't. I'll get them." She walked slowly from the room.

"It's so sad," Betty said.

Mary nodded. "I wish we'd had better news for her."

Elle returned, carrying a small wooden box. "I keep them in here. Just a few keepsakes." She opened the lid and gazed down into the box, a smile tweaking her lips. "We sent a lot of notes back and forth, and any time one of us went away, we'd write letters."

Mary looked into the box and saw a neat pile of envelopes and folded sheets of paper. The top one was a slip of lined paper from a small notebook. "See you at 3," she read. Below the words was a simple drawing. Mary caught her breath. "What is that?"

"What?" Elle asked.

Mary took out the note and pointed to the drawing. "This same symbol was on the note that said 'To Elle' on the painting."

Elle laughed. "That's Maude's sign. We had sort of a code when we were girls, and we each had a sign for our names. Here, I'll show you." She strode to the counter and set down the box, then took up a pen and a small shopping-list pad. "This is Maude's sign, and here's mine." She quickly sketched two symbols on the paper.

"Those were both on the letter she left you in the back of the painting."

"Yes, we had used them for years by that time. Seeing them today...well, it gave me hope. The fact that she used them meant she wasn't as angry with me as I'd feared."

Betty leaned in to look at the pad. "You must have had a lot of fun together as girls."

"Are there other signs in the code?" Mary asked.

"Land, yes. You'll likely see some if you read these notes. We kept adding new signs as we went along. For instance, there was a teacher we particularly disliked. We had a sign we used instead of his name, so that if anyone else saw the notes, they wouldn't know who we were talking about." Elle jotted on the pad for a moment. "There, that's Mr. Ledbetter. You may see it in the notes. Oh, and here's one that meant 'meet me.' We could make this sign and write a number after it—meet me at 7—that sort of thing." She tore off the top sheet of the shopping list.

Mary took the paper and put it in the box with the letters and notes. "Do you remember others?"

"I might, if I thought about it. Tell you what, if you need to know one, you can call me. I might not remember it, but I'll try."

"Thanks." Mary glanced at Betty. "I suppose we'd better head home."

"Yes, we should. Thank you for the tea and the recipe." Betty smiled at Elle.

"You're welcome. It's you ladies who've done the favor. Thanks for driving all this way and bringing me the painting. And the letter, of course. That's probably just as important. I'll treasure them both." Elle walked over to the table and looked down at Maude's painting again. "I can't tell you how glad I am to know she wanted me to have this."

Mary took the box of notes with her to the bookshop on Monday, along with a box of Uncle Lew's papers she had yet to sort. Brooding clouds had drifted in from the west, and she suspected the threat of snow would keep a lot of shoppers home today.

Her hunch proved right, and she and Rebecca had no customers during the first hour. Mary caught up on her financial records while Rebecca straightened and dusted everything in sight. By eleven o'clock, Mary was free to work on her mystery. As she opened the box of Elle's notes, she considered giving Rebecca the rest of the day off. But if she did that, customers might arrive when she had her papers spread out and was immersed in deciphering the old letters.

The door opened, admitting a gust of cold air along with Henry Woodrow.

"Hi, Henry," Rebecca called. "Is it snowing?"

"Not yet." Henry shut the door firmly and pulled off his hat as he walked smiling toward the counter. "How are you ladies doing on this freezing day?"

"We're fine." Mary smiled and nodded toward the box of papers. "As you can see, business is a bit slow, and I'm puttering at something else."

"A new mystery to solve?" Henry's gray eyebrows shot up. "Tell me about it."

"I'd love to. Would you like a cup of tea while we talk?"

"Better and better," Henry said.

He chatted easily with Rebecca while Mary went into the back room to prepare the tea. She carried two steaming mugs out a few minutes later, and Henry joined her in the cozy area near the fieldstone fireplace.

Mary switched on the gas fire and called, "Rebecca, would you like tea? There's more hot water."

"No, you two go ahead. I'll finish this."

Mary couldn't imagine what "this" was, as they'd taken care of everything that needed doing. She suspected Rebecca was giving her some time to talk to Henry uninterrupted.

"Haven't seen much of you lately." Henry blew on the surface of his tea and took an experimental sip.

"I've been pretty busy since my Uncle Lew died. I told you about Betty and I inheriting his house, and we've been dealing with that. In fact, those papers I was working on are connected to Uncle Lew and Aunt Maude."

"Sounds like a big job."

Mary nodded, frowning. "It's led to a bit of a mystery."

Henry smiled. "I'm all ears."

For the next few minutes, Mary laid out the tale, starting with Uncle Lew's will and ending with their trip to Elle Weir's house, filling in all the details she hadn't told him earlier.

"There's so much confusion surrounding Aunt Maude's death—or perhaps I should say her disappearance. Now I'm not even sure she died then, funeral or no funeral."

"It does seem a bit odd, that funeral."

Mary took a sip of her cooling tea and set her mug down. "It was a memorial service, really. No body. It was held a few weeks after the unidentified body washed ashore, and I have to assume Uncle Lew thought it was Aunt Maude's body. Maybe the preliminary reports made it seem conclusive."

"But later they learned otherwise?"

She shrugged. "I've heard that, but I don't have the official word yet. Chief McArthur is trying to find out about it for me—in his spare time."

"Ha!" Henry grinned, but quickly sobered. "Does that make you feel like your uncle was rushing things a bit?"

"Sort of. I mean, why not wait for definite evidence?"

"They didn't have the benefit of DNA tests back then." Henry's eyebrows drew together in a frown. "Sometimes people need closure. If he'd been wondering what happened to her and then waiting weeks on this drowning thing...well, I'm just saying."

"Yes, it could be that way." Mary still had doubts in the recesses of her mind.

Henry cocked his head to one side. "You're thinking maybe he knew something about her death, and he was overeager to convince other people she was dead? Maybe get them to put it behind them, so he could do the same?"

"I hate to even think it," Mary admitted. She jumped up from her chair. "I've got the guest book from the memorial service here. Would you take a look at it? Sometimes an impartial pair of eyes sees things the people closest to the situation don't notice."

"Be happy to." Henry drained his mug and set it on the coffee table.

Mary went to the counter and opened the box of Uncle Lew's papers. She had put the guest book in on top at the last minute, in case she found other items in the box that would show a connection to some of the memorial guests.

She handed the book to Henry, and he opened it to the first page. Mary sat down and watched as he browsed through it. After flipping several pages, he paused and scrutinized one. She figured he was reading the signatures of the guests.

"I don't see my folks' names in here."

"Did they know Uncle Lew and Aunt Maude well?"

"They must have known them, but I'm not sure how well. Still, back then, it seemed the whole community turned out for funerals."

Mary nodded, puzzling over that. "It was held in Provincetown, not here. They'd lived out on the Cape for several years."

"I see." Henry turned the page and continued studying the names. "I recognize some of these names. Your folks, of course, and your grandparents."

"Yes, all of the Nelson family seems to have turned out to support Uncle Lew. Henry, do you suppose…"

He looked up. "What?"

"Well, it's true they'd lived in Provincetown awhile—four or five years—but most of their friends and relatives still lived in Ivy Bay. It's only sixty miles or so. Why do you suppose he had the service out there, not here in town?"

Henry seemed to think that over. "I suppose it was more convenient for him."

"Yes, but harder for everyone else."

"You're thinking maybe…" Henry frowned and shifted in his chair. "Maybe Lew *wanted* fewer people there?"

"I'm not sure," Mary said. "If he truly didn't want to call attention to her death, why have a service at all? But if he was trying to convince people she'd died when really she'd left him, why not hold it in Ivy Bay, where more people knew them?"

"I can't answer that, unless he really believed she was dead and was so grief-stricken he did what seemed easiest."

"The path of least resistance." She nodded slowly. "I suppose that's the most comfortable explanation. I do wish I could ask Mom and Dad about it."

"Well, I see that the old pastor of Grace Church spoke at the service."

"Really? I wasn't sure, and Betty didn't recognize the name."

"He preached here when I was a kid," Henry said.

"We must have heard him in the summer, then. I guess it wasn't that memorable an experience."

Henry chuckled. "Well, he retired when I was...oh, eight or nine, I'm guessing. No reason why you should remember him, really."

"I suppose he's dead now."

"Oh yeah. He was old back then."

"Do you recognize any other names in the book, other than my family?"

"Well, sure. There's William Benner. He's still living. He must have been pretty young then."

They went through the list, and Mary wrote down the names of people Henry thought might still be alive and living in the area. She was left with only two Ivy Bay residents and one who listed Provincetown as his residence in the guest book. Mary had brought Uncle Lew's Provincetown phone directory home with her, and she located the name in the book.

"I can check the others listed in Provincetown," she said. "There may be more people who are still around and remember Aunt Maude."

"They'd have been kids or young adults then," Henry said, shaking his head.

"It's not much to go on, but it's all I've got at this point—a handful of elderly people."

Henry handed the book across to her. "Guess I'd better shove off."

"Thanks for coming by," Mary said. "And thanks for your help."

"Didn't do much."

"Talking things over with you always helps."

ELEVEN

That afternoon, Mary pursued the new leads she had. One of the women who had attended the memorial service had been moved to a nursing home and was too frail for a visit from a stranger. Her daughter explained to Mary that her mother probably wouldn't remember those long-ago events anyway. Mary thanked her and tried the next name on her list.

William Benner spoke to Mary on the phone. He lived in a retirement village in Hyannis. He remembered Lew Nelson and Mary's father, Davis, but couldn't recall any details about Maude's death or the memorial service.

The man from Provincetown proved to be a former coworker of Lew's. He had shared a desk in the same office for a while, though he quit working with Lew a year later and opened a bed-and-breakfast with his wife.

"Sure, I went to the funeral," he told Mary. "It was pretty grim."

Mary wished she could see his face, but she couldn't see driving all the way to Provincetown again so soon, unless she had more clues to follow up on. "How do you mean?" she asked.

"For one thing, they just had a picture of her. No casket or anything. Flowers, of course."

"Did you know Maude personally?"

"I'd met her a few times. She was pretty. And artistic, you know. She liked to paint."

"Yes, she did."

"*Hmm*, well, I wouldn't want to say anything bad about the dead."

"About my Aunt Maude, you mean?"

"I was thinking of him. Lew Nelson."

Mary swallowed hard. "You know something bad about Lew?"

"Oh, I don't *know* anything. There was talk at the time though."

"What sort of talk?" Mary braced herself to hear the worst.

"Well, some folks said he treated his wife bad and she drowned herself. There were even rumors that he'd killed her, but he was never arrested or anything. Sorry—hope I didn't upset you."

"No, I'm not upset. I want to know what people thought. But even more, I want to know what really happened. And I hope to find out."

"I don't expect he really killed her," the man said evenly. "Of course, Lew did have a bad temper when he was young, but I thought he mellowed as he got older. They never found her body, though, did they?"

"I...I don't know. I'm hoping the police can find the old records for me." Mary decided she'd gotten all the facts she could from this man, and she didn't want to listen to more of his speculation. "Thank you very much for talking to me."

"No problem."

She hung up and sat scowling at the phone for several seconds. What had begun as a fun exercise to satisfy her curiosity was becoming more serious. She knew she couldn't be satisfied now if she didn't find out the truth.

Rebecca came from the back room carrying a carton in her arms. "I almost forgot about these new Bobbsey Twin reprints. Do you want to make a display in the children's area?"

"Yes, let's do that." Mary put the memorial-service guest book back into the box and closed the telephone book. "I think I've done enough sleuthing for the day. It's getting depressing."

Rebecca smiled in sympathy. "I was going to point out that it's snowing now, but I didn't want to make you feel worse. It's definitely time for something fun."

Mary joined her in the children's corner. "Let's use this table. I'm not sure why I'm so driven to investigate Aunt Maude's death."

"Because it puts a bad light on your family." Rebecca opened the flaps of the carton.

"Maybe so. I would like to prove that Uncle Lew didn't cause Aunt Maude's death. That just doesn't fit with the uncle I knew. He seemed fairly mild-mannered and quiet. Maybe living alone for sixty years does that to you. Or maybe I just never spent enough time with him to know the real Lew."

Later, when it was nearly closing time, she surveyed the bookshop with mixed feelings. Everything looked wonderful—cozy and inviting—from the Bobbsey Twins display to the latest Cape Cod murder mystery. But they'd only had half a dozen customers all day, including Henry. Maybe it was foolish to stay open on these short, gray winter days.

The snow fell sporadically and so far was barely sticking to the pavement. On her way home, Mary stopped at the police station. The civilian secretary told her she was in luck because the chief had stayed late. She took Mary to his office.

"Hello, Mary." The chief rose and smiled wearily. "I'm sorry I haven't had a chance to look for those records for you. We've been busy, but I still plan to do it."

"Thanks. I wonder if I can add a little bit to the request."

"What's on your mind?"

Mary sat down, and Chief McArthur sank back into his swivel chair.

"I told you before that some people thought the drowning victim was my great-aunt Maude Nelson. Well, I'm leaning toward believing it wasn't her. But if it's not…well, I'd sure like to know how she did die, and when. Nobody seems to know for sure. I've got a lot of my uncle's papers, but so far I haven't found a death certificate or anything like that. My inquiries at the county clerk's office and online haven't turned up a death record for her either. I'm starting to think her body was never found. And that makes me wonder if she really died when the family thought she did. If she was still alive when that memorial service was held, when did she really die?"

"Huh. Interesting." The chief tipped his chair back and studied her face. "What do you think happened?"

"I wish I knew. The most likely scenario is that she left my uncle and he was too embarrassed to admit it. But I've heard rumors of murder."

"I'll surely check on it. I'll try to do it soon too." He sat forward and scribbled a note on a memo pad.

"If she did leave him and moved to another state, I suppose I wouldn't find her death record easily," Mary mused.

"That's a possibility, I guess. Sorry to keep you waiting so long on this thing. If you can come back in a couple of days, I'll try to have something for you."

"Thank you," Mary said. "If Uncle Lew was suspected of killing his wife—officially, I mean—then I'd like to know. I want to know the truth, Chief. And I hope we can set the record straight."

Chief McArthur nodded soberly. "I'll help if I can."

The next morning, Pastor Frank Miles came into the bookshop with his grandson, Trevor.

"Well, hello," Mary called cheerfully. "Glad to see folks are getting out this morning."

"It's bright and sunny today," the pastor said. "Quite a change from yesterday."

Trevor scowled. "I wish we got more snow."

"Snow is lots of fun for boys," Pastor Miles said, "but not so good for people who have to drive around in it."

"I have a book I think you'd like, Trevor." Mary led them into the children's section. "Tell me if you've read it before, but I don't think you have." She picked up a copy of *The Bobbsey Twins at Snow Lodge* from the display. "These are very old books that have been reprinted."

"Oh yes, you like the Bobbsey Twins," Pastor Miles said.

"They're okay," Trevor said doubtfully.

"I suppose they seem very old-fashioned to you." Mary looked at the pastor.

"We've read two, and I know *I* enjoyed them. You liked Bert a lot, didn't you, Trevor?"

"He's okay."

Mary chuckled. "Well, I do have some more recent books. In fact, an author living not too far from here has started a series for children. I don't think any of them have snow in them though." She took down a volume and held it out.

Trevor eyed the cover cautiously. A boy and a girl were pictured riding bicycles down a hill path, with a small dog running beside them. He reached for the book.

"That's the first one," Mary said to the pastor. "Here's the next in the series, if you'd like to take a look. I read the one Trevor's holding, and it's a cute story. I know Ashley enjoyed it too." Again, Mary wished Ashley could be at the store more often.

"I'll take your word and Ashley's," Pastor Miles said.

By this time, Trevor was seated on the carpet, turning the first few pages of the book.

"I have an unrelated question for you," Mary said to the pastor. "I've been looking through some things from my Uncle Lew's house. I told you about him—"

"Yes. You said you and Betty were responsible for his house."

"That's one way to put it. We've been looking into what happened to his wife—our Aunt Maude. She died in 1950, and apparently the pastor of Grace Church spoke at the memorial service, even though it was held in Provincetown."

"Why did they use an Ivy Bay pastor?"

"They grew up here, and the family went to Grace Church in the old days. The pastor and his wife signed the guest book from the memorial service, and a notation of 'and family' is included. Obviously, the pastor and his wife have long since passed away, but I wondered about their children."

"*Hmm*, I think they had a couple of daughters. One, at least, is still living. She's in her mid-seventies. She visited the church two or three years ago. She lives in Barnstable now."

"I don't suppose you have an address?" Mary asked.

"I do—and a phone number as well. We thought we'd do something to honor the church's former pastors when the next major anniversary comes up, and Mrs. Levalle asked me to notify her of that. I could call you with her number after we get home."

"Thank you! I'm trying to speak to as many people as possible who attended Aunt Maude's service."

"Sounds like a mystery to me," Pastor Miles said.

"Sort of. There's a lot of confusion about how and when my great-aunt died."

He smiled. "That glitter in your eyes always gives you away. I'll give you a buzz." He turned and called, "Trevor, are we getting that book?"

———

Betty's book club met the next day, but she encouraged Mary to drive to Barnstable to see Mrs. Levalle, the daughter of Grace Church's former pastor, without her. Mary arranged the meeting by phone. When she mentioned her bookshop,

Mrs. Levalle revealed that she loved cozy mysteries, and so Mary chose a gift for her from her inventory.

The hostess and her husband, who was a retired contractor, were both at home and greeted Mary cordially.

"I brought you this." Mary held out the book. "I hope it's one you haven't read."

"No, I haven't, but it looks exciting." Mrs. Levalle's face shone with pleasure as she surveyed the cover. "Won't you come sit down? I've fixed coffee."

For several minutes, they talked about Ivy Bay, and Mary brought the couple up to date on happenings at Grace Church. When she mentioned Uncle Lew and Aunt Maude, Mrs. Levalle nodded soberly.

"I remember them. Maude was so pretty and so young! It was quite a tragedy."

"I believe you went to the memorial service with your parents," Mary said.

"Yes, and my sister Linda went along too. We'd both known Maude. Of course, she and her husband had moved out of town." Her face clouded. "It was quite odd, what happened after."

"After?" Mary prompted.

"I guess you know they didn't find her body."

"I'd heard that. Some say she drowned."

"Some did say that. But some of us wondered." Mrs. Levalle glanced at her husband.

"You may as well tell it," he said, and promptly took a swallow of his coffee.

"It's nothing, really," Mrs. Levalle said. "I was young— only thirteen or fourteen—and everyone said I was mistaken. Perhaps I was."

Mary's skin prickled in anticipation. "About what?"

Mrs. Levalle let out a deep sigh. "I thought I saw her. But I couldn't have, could I? It was a month or more after the funeral, so how could I?" She raised her chin and looked Mary in the eye. "I don't believe in ghosts."

"Neither do I," Mary said. "Tell me about it."

"I was walking to my friend's house after supper. It was in the fall, either late October or early November. There was still some light—twilight we'd call it back then. And I saw her come out of the gallery."

Mary blinked. "The Ivy Bay Gallery?"

"Yes. I can't remember what it was called then, but I was sure I saw her. She ducked into the alley between it and the next building. When I got even with the alley, she was gone. I told my friend about it and scared her to death. Her mother said I was imagining things."

"What did your parents say?"

She shook her head slowly. "They agreed I'd seen something. *Someone.* Papa said it was probably a woman with a similar appearance—blonde hair like Maude's, and she had a lean, lithe build. But they didn't think it could have been Maude Nelson."

"Did you do anything about it?" Mary asked.

"My father went to the gallery the next day and asked the owner about it. He said he'd had quite a few customers the previous day, but he couldn't recall one who looked much like Maude Nelson. Papa told me to forget it. It was probably a combination of my imagination and the recent tragedy."

"But you think it was her."

"I don't know what I think now," Mrs. Levalle said. "My friend insisted it was Maude's ghost. My sister and I cooked up a story that might explain it. A foolish tale of a long-lost twin or some such thing. Ridiculous, but we were children." Mary nodded. "If it's any comfort, I've researched her family, and Maude didn't have any sisters."

"I thought not. And when we heard that the drowning victim wasn't her—well, I just don't know. But for what it's worth, that's what happened."

Mr. Levalle cleared his throat. "My wife first told me about that incident a few years after we were married. I always thought it was interesting, but we've never reached a conclusion. My best guess is that your aunt was still alive, and that she was in Ivy Bay. I don't think that was any apparition my wife saw."

———

Betty met Mary at the kitchen door when she returned home, her blue eyes wide with portent.

"You'll never guess what I learned today."

Mary smiled and pulled off her gloves. "I have news too. You go first."

"All right. We held the book club meeting at Virginia Livingston's house today. We were there once before, but we held it in the living room. Today she took us into the sunroom. I'd never seen it before."

Mary paused in removing her coat. "I'm guessing this has to do with Aunt Maude."

"Bingo. Virginia has one of Aunt Maude's paintings hanging in her sunroom."

TWELVE

◆◆◆

Virginia smiled graciously when she opened her door to Mary that evening. "Hello, Mary. Come right in."

"Thanks so much for letting me come on short notice." Mary stepped inside. "When Betty told me about your painting, I was so excited! I can't wait to see it."

Virginia's eyes twinkled. "You're welcome to have a look. May I take your coat?"

"Thank you." Mary shrugged out of it and handed it to her.

Virginia hung her coat in a closet off the entry and then returned to Mary's side. "I don't think I've ever seen your sister so animated. She seems to think I have quite a treasure." As she spoke, she led Mary into a cozy room with a pitched ceiling and large windows on the south and east sides.

"Betty probably told you about the paintings we inherited," Mary said, looking around. She spotted Aunt Maude's work immediately, on the west wall, and stepped toward it.

"Yes. She said yours all depict Provincetown, where Mrs. Nelson lived later. As you can see, mine is an Ivy Bay scene."

"How charming!" Mary gazed at the scene depicting the Seafarers' Hall and the waterfront beyond. "I think this must be one of her earlier works. The detail doesn't seem quite as refined, but it has the same whimsical quality as the others."

She found herself scanning the tiny figures in the painting, but none of them looked familiar. After a moment, she realized she was looking for the red-haired man, but he wasn't there.

"Has this painting been in your family long?"

"My parents bought it at the gallery, here in Ivy Bay, in 1948. I have the receipt."

"Oh, wonderful," Mary said.

"Yes, I found it in Dad's papers when I settled his estate. They must have been the original owners."

"Aunt Maude did sell her paintings through the gallery then. Would you mind if I snapped a couple of photos with my cell phone, so I can compare it to the ones we have?"

"I guess not."

Mary snapped a frame, stepped closer, and clicked again. She hoped the lighting was good enough for her to see the details in the photo when she transferred it to her computer. She took one more shot, focusing in on the signature.

"Well, thank you. This was a real treat." She stepped back and pocketed her phone.

"You're welcome," Virginia said.

Mary took her leave and drove home wondering if this helped her investigation or not. It was fun knowing some of Aunt Maude's earlier work was out there and that a local resident owned and treasured one of her Ivy Bay paintings.

Mary called Rebecca in the morning and told her that she would be late coming to the bookshop. She drove downtown and parked outside the Ivy Bay Gallery.

Mason Willoughby was waiting on a customer, and Mary browsed the shop while she waited. He had a variety of paintings on display—some coastal New England scenics, a few abstracts, and some interesting still lifes. Two portraits of children were showcased on one wall, and Mary was caught by their vivacity.

When the customer left, Mason joined her.

"Hello, Mrs. Fisher. I see you're drawn to Ned Upton's paintings."

"I like them very much," Mary said. "Have you had a chance to look through those old records?"

"I have, and I think you'll be pleased. I found the former owner's ledger for 1945 to 1950."

Mary's pulse surged. "Wonderful! May I see it?"

"Of course." Mason led her to the checkout, where he stooped and took an old, tall ledger from beneath the counter. "They had cash registers then, but the owner kept records of his consignees in this book. His name was James Ludwig, and he owned the gallery for about twenty-five years. This ledger has records of all the artwork that passed through the gallery during the postwar years and payments he made to the consignees. It also has his end-of-the year inventories, which I found very interesting."

"I'd love to study it." Mary had packed a notebook, in case he was reluctant to let her take the book out of the building, but he smiled and held it out to her.

"I know you're a conscientious person and that you'll handle it carefully. I wouldn't mind if you borrowed it for a few days."

"Oh, thank you, Mr. Willoughby! That's very generous of you. I promise to take good care of it and to bring it back soon."

"Shall we say in a couple of weeks?"

"That's perfect."

Mr. Willoughby nodded. "Very good. I'll see you next week, then."

⸻

Mary spent more than an hour that evening combing through the old ledger and making notes as she went. Almost immediately, she could see that Maude had displayed her paintings regularly on consignment at the gallery while she lived in Ivy Bay. She may even have done so before the time period covered by the ledger, but she certainly continued during those years. In fact, she kept on selling through the Ivy Bay Gallery after she moved to Provincetown.

Mary blinked several times as she turned one of the final pages. She promised herself a cup of tea once she reached the end of the listings.

She passed the date of Maude's memorial service and skimmed through the rest, not expecting any more entries under the Nelson name. To her surprise, a notation for October 23, 1950, showed a payment to Maude Nelson. Mary bent close over the ledger and read it again. She checked the dates above and below it. Could this be a mistake?

She scrunched her eyes shut tight and opened them again. Mary's heart pounded wildly. This payment coincided with Mrs. Levalle's supposed sighting of Maude near the gallery.

"Betty," she called.

Betty poked her head through the kitchen doorway. "What is it?"

"Come take a look at this, if you have a moment. Tell me what you think." Mary showed her the entry and explained how it dovetailed with the story given by the pastor's daughter.

"Well." Betty stared down at the ledger. "Why don't you ask Mason about it?"

"He wasn't even sure these records existed until I had him look for them," Mary protested.

"But he might know the vagaries of paying a consignment artist."

Mary saw the sense of that and put a call through to Mr. Willoughby. He answered his home phone, and she quickly explained what she had found in the ledger. "That was more than a month after her memorial service. How would you explain that? I mean, is it possible?"

"I can think of one way it might have happened," he said easily. "Lew Nelson may have gone to the gallery after she died to collect the paintings she had on display there and any money that was due her. Check the inventory for the end of the year."

Mary turned to the end of the book and skimmed down the pages, looking for "Nelson."

"I don't see any of her paintings listed in December, 1950," she said.

"Okay, go back to the page where you found the payment and look down from there."

"Oh, here we go," Mary said slowly. "A few lines down, it says, 'Two harbor scenes, M. Nelson, removed.' Is that what you're talking about?"

"Yes. It sounds to me as though James Ludwig removed her last two paintings from his inventory. He probably returned them to your uncle."

"It doesn't say." Mary quickly searched the rest of the November and December listings. "I don't see anything else after that."

"There you go." Mason sounded almost cheerful. "Her husband probably claimed them, and Mr. Ludwig paid him for any that had sold before he came in."

"I guess that makes sense," Mary said, still thinking of the teenage girl who thought she saw Maude Nelson about that time.

After she and Mr. Willoughby hung up, she told Betty what she had learned.

"I think that makes sense too," Betty said.

"But what about Mrs. Levalle's sighting?"

Betty shrugged. "We'll never know, will we?"

"I suppose not." Mary pressed her lips together. At a sudden thought, she turned back to Betty. "The ledger says two harbor scenes. Do you think those could be two of the paintings we found in Uncle Lew's attic?"

"I don't know. One of them I'd call a harbor scene, but one was more a beach scene, and the others were views of the village. And they were in Provincetown, remember. Would she sell Provincetown paintings in Ivy Bay? Seems more likely to me that she'd put Ivy Bay scenes in the gallery here."

Mary thought about that. "Maybe after she moved, all her paintings were of Provincetown. I mean, if Uncle Lew took back two Ivy Bay harbor scenes, why didn't we find them in his house with the rest? I hate to give up on the idea that Aunt Maude returned to the gallery in October to pick up her payment and the leftover paintings."

"If she did," Betty said slowly, "then the gallery owner knew she wasn't dead."

"Yeah." Mary stared at her sister. "What if *he* was the mystery man in Aunt Maude's life?"

"The one person she could trust?" Betty asked.

"Yes." Mary turned that over in her mind. "Nobody else admitted seeing her after her death. The pastor's daughter was the only one, and everyone else told her that she had imagined it. But if it was true, then this man knew about it, and he kept his mouth shut."

"I'm not saying it's true," Betty said cautiously. "But if it were, he'd have to have a good reason."

"That's what I think. He didn't want anyone to know she'd been there. Therefore, we can assume he didn't want anyone to know she was still alive."

"Can we really assume that?" Betty shook her head. "It seems like a leap to me. That man must be dead by now. How can we know what his motive was?"

"I'm going to investigate him, starting tomorrow." Mary closed the ledger. "I can at least find out if he was married at the time. And if he was, I can look for a divorce record."

Betty's lips twitched, and she looked slightly ill. "You don't really think Aunt Maude broke up another marriage?"

"I don't know what to think. But I'm keeping an open mind."

———

The following evening, Mary examined the four paintings of Aunt Maude's that now belonged to her and Betty. The bookshop had been quite busy that day, and Rebecca had left her at two o'clock to take Ashley to a dental appointment. Afterward, Ashley had joined them at the shop for a couple of hours. Mary hadn't had much time to investigate, other than a cursory check on the previous gallery owner, James Ludwig. She hadn't found much, except confirmation that he had lived in Ivy Bay and run the gallery there during the 1940s and '50s. She would have to do some serious digging into his personal life when she had time.

As she studied the paintings in the spare bedroom, she jotted notes about the people in them. The red-haired man was an obvious recurring character. Was it possible there were others that she and Betty hadn't noticed? When she tired of moving back and forth between the paintings, she took them down and laid them in a line on the bed. Starting with the one that had the fewest people, she chose one figure at a time and searched for that person in the other paintings.

She found several that were similar but not definitely the same. At the end of half an hour, she had found only one other repeat—a young woman with flowing blonde hair. In both the beach scene and the picnic painting, she wore a blue-and-yellow sundress. Mary studied that dress carefully and decided her discovery was worth carrying the two paintings downstairs.

She stood them up on the sofa before she went and knocked on Betty's door.

"Come in," Betty called.

"Hi." Mary opened the door slightly. "I hope I'm not disturbing you."

"No, I'm just writing a letter."

Mary stepped into the room. "I found something in the paintings that I'd like your opinion on. Could you come out to the living room for a minute?"

"Sure." Betty rose slowly. "I should move around a bit anyway. I get so stiff."

In the living room, Mary pointed to the young woman in the beach scene. "Notice anything peculiar about her?"

Betty gazed at the figure for a moment and caught her breath. "It's the dress, isn't it? The one I brought home."

"I think so." Mary waited while Betty absorbed that.

"Do you think it's a self-portrait?"

"That occurred to me." Mary stepped closer to the second painting. "Now look over here." She waved in the general area of a group of women who were setting out food on a picnic table.

Betty cocked her head toward her shoulder and frowned. "What am I looking for? Oh!" She gasped and bent closer. "It's her!"

"It sure is," Mary said. "Look closely."

"Oh my." Betty raised her chin and stared at Mary. "Is she..."

Mary nodded. "She's pregnant."

"But—" Betty looked at the painting again, then back to the beach scene. "Aunt Maude and Uncle Lew didn't have any children."

THIRTEEN

———◆◆◆———

Mary replaced the paintings in the guest room and then took the packet of notes and letters Elle had given her and went downstairs. She settled near the fireplace and slowly read through them. Most were short notes that sounded very girlish. "I have to go right home after school." "Can you go to the beach with me tomorrow?"

One note had a symbol that Mary assumed stood for a name. It was followed by "is thinking of enlisting." She wished the notes were dated, but she assumed that one was written in the early days of the war.

She opened one longer letter, which Maude had apparently written while on a trip with her parents. Mary laughed as she read about the family's visit to an elderly cousin of Maude's father—a woman Maude apparently found repellant. "She served lemonade so watery it was more like sour water," the girl complained. Later, she said, "Tomorrow we are supposed to see the Liberty Bell. I want to go to the Philly Museum of Art, but Mama says we might not have time. Woe! That is the only thing that has made this trip tolerable. I'll be so upset if I don't get to go." Mary had to smile at the young woman's dramatic flair.

She looked at the envelope. It had a postmark, so this letter, at least, could be dated. In 1938, the Price family had made their trip to Philadelphia. She sincerely hoped that Maude was able to go to the museum.

As she read, Mary listed the "code" symbols she found. She had about twenty when she finished, and knew the meanings of about half. Elle had told her a few, and she figured out others from the context. Two had the meaning written in. For one of those, Maude had written, "He has a mouth like a fish. Use this:" followed by a small fish drawing in a triangle. The derogatory line referred to a math teacher. Maude appeared to resent his homework assignments.

Several symbols represented names or whole words, while others seemed to represent individual letters. She found one example that she was sure meant something like "alert" or "danger," and the symbols were such that they could transliterate into "SOS." She figured out drawings that had to mean "school" and "meet" or "meeting place." Maude's name symbol consisted of their code letter *M* combined with another mark. After much puzzling, Mary decided that Elle's name was simply their symbol for the letter *L*.

Betty came from her room and paused in the doorway. "Are you forgetting our art class this evening?"

Mary looked up. "Oh, you're right! It slipped my mind." Mary put the letters back in the box and stood.

"I've been thinking about Aunt Maude's family, and I was hoping you could show me how to look them up online."

Betty glanced at her watch. "We can try. We have a few minutes. It's usually harder to get information on recent generations than it is on older ones. But I can check some of the big family-history sites and see if anyone has posted files on that branch of the Price clan."

"That'd be great."

They went to Betty's computer. With the information Mary had gathered from Aunt Maude and Uncle Lew's wedding announcement and the memorial-service book, Betty was able to locate the Price family in the 1940 census.

"This is the newest census released to the public," Betty said. "They only release them after seventy-two years."

"It's perfect for our purposes. Aunt Maude and Uncle Lew got married in 1943." Mary watched the screen eagerly as Betty brought up the information on the family group. "Mother and two children. Maude Ruth was seventeen, and it looks as though she had a big brother."

"Yes," Betty murmured. "He was nineteen in 1940."

"I wonder if he went into the military." Mary told her about the note in Elle's packet that said someone was thinking of enlisting.

"Let's see if we can find him on another site." Betty clicked to her favorites list and went to a site specializing in information on veterans. "Oh! Bad news."

Mary read the information on the screen. "He was killed in Italy. What a shame."

"Poor Maude. I wonder what happened to their father."

"We can look at the 1930 census and see if he was there." Betty clicked through various screens until the family's census information came up for a decade earlier than they had viewed before.

"He was alive and living with the family then," Mary noted.

After a few more minutes of searching, Betty was able to establish that Maude's father had died in 1938.

"What about her mom?" Mary asked. "She was alive at the time of the wedding. Can we find out if she was still around when Maude disappeared?"

"We can try."

Mary watched as Betty clicked the keys. She soon found an obituary for Maude's mother, dated 1948.

"That poor girl," Betty said.

"All alone except for Uncle Lew." Mary's spirits drooped just thinking about it. How could she have survived the tragedies in her life without Betty and the rest of her family? "There are so few people left who knew her." She sighed. "I guess it's time to go over to the church."

"I do hope all this work you're doing pays off," Betty said as she closed the computer program. "Even if Aunt Maude's been dead more than sixty years, it would be good if we could know what really happened to her."

———

Betty had bought a set of new watercolor brushes and was eager to try them out at the class. Mary could see that painting might become a lifelong hobby for her sister.

"Doesn't Brooke look darling?" she whispered to Betty as they entered the church hall. Their teacher was wearing a red maternity dress with flowered accents and a cream-colored cardigan.

They began to set up for the class. When Brooke came over to greet them, Mary said, "You look cozy and warm, Brooke. I love your dress."

"Thanks. My mom bought me this outfit, and I *do* like it."

Mary wondered at her choice of words—as if there had been some doubt about her feelings for the new clothing. She glanced around to see if Brooke's mother had come tonight. Sure enough, Linda was busy unloading a tray of cups at the refreshment table.

Another student came in and went straight to Brooke. "How are you feeling?"

"Pretty well," Brooke said, smiling.

Mary noticed that Linda's chin shot up, and she gazed across the room to where Brooke was giving the newcomer an account of her latest activities. Mary hurried across to the refreshment table.

"Hi, Linda. Do you need any help tonight?"

"Oh, thank you, Mary, but I'm all set. Doesn't Brooke look lovely tonight?"

"She sure does. A new outfit always perks a girl up."

Linda leaned close. "I bought it for her, you know."

"That was so nice of you. She told me how much she likes it." Linda opened her mouth again, and Mary said quickly, "Are you going to paint tonight? I loved what you did at the first class."

"No, I've decided that I'm better in the hostess role than I am behind an easel."

"I see. What did you bring us tonight?"

Mary kept her chatting another moment or two, until Brooke stepped over to her own easel. She hurried back to her spot. She'd have to be quick now to get her things out, but at least Brooke had been able to greet the students without interference.

Betty eyed her placidly as Brooke gave her introductory remarks. They would do some sketching in the first part of the class, focusing on balance in their composition. Afterward, they could paint any subject they wished, but they had to apply what they had learned.

"I think I'll ask Linda if I can paint her teapot tonight," Betty said.

"Her teapot?" Mary stretched her neck so she could see it. The blue-and-white pot sat in the place of honor in the middle of the food table. "That's pretty. I didn't notice it before. It doesn't belong to the church, does it?"

"No, it's an antique. She must have brought it from home. I'll ask her about it."

Mary smiled. She and Betty could tag-team Linda successfully, she was sure. Not that she wanted to keep Linda from ever talking about the baby, but Brooke showed a lot less stress when her mom was otherwise occupied.

As she worked on her sketches, Mary overheard snatches of conversation. Brooke made her rounds of the room, commenting on the students' work, and several asked her about the baby. Mary decided to paint a baby's cradle tonight. It would make a nice composition, though it might be too complicated for her to finish tonight. She sketched it sitting on a braided rug, with the corner of a small quilt peeping over the edge of the wooden cradle.

"I like that," Brooke said with enthusiasm as she looked down at Mary's sketchbook.

"Thanks. I admit you inspired it."

Brooke laughed and patted her stomach. "Have fun with it." She started to turn away, then came back to Mary's side.

"Say, didn't you tell me you hoped to find more of your aunt's paintings?"

"I'd love to know if there are more out there," Mary agreed. "Betty learned that her friend Virginia Livingston has one, and I've been to her house to see it."

"I know a couple of Web sites you could use to search for the artist's name," Brooke said. "If artwork goes on the market, lots of times it's listed on these sites, and often there'll be a thumbnail photo of the painting so that bidders can see it."

"That sounds wonderful," Mary said.

"I'll e-mail you the information," Brooke said.

Betty had moved her easel closer to the refreshment table and was working in earnest on her still life that included the teapot.

Mary worked away in silence, concentrating on the lines of the cradle. The quilt could droop and sag, but the wooden side of the cradle had to be straight. At last, she got the edge the way she wanted it. The grain lines in the wood could curve a little, so her hand needn't be so steady for the rest.

As she painted, she thought about the upcoming baby shower. Of course, Brooke's mother would be there. She hoped the committee could keep it a secret from Linda until the last minute, though they had agreed that they might need to enlist her help to make sure Brooke kept the evening of the shower free.

Mary began to think about all Linda had done for Brooke and Bill. It was true she sometimes seemed to overdo her attentions, but the young couple must appreciate all her thoughtful touches. Maybe a special gift for Linda was in order.

The more Mary thought about that idea, the more she liked it. Linda would feel honored if she received a gift meant just for her. The right item came to Mary's mind as she painted in splotches of pink on the baby quilt in her picture. It would go perfectly with the art theme of the shower. She would make an album for Linda that held prints of famous paintings, all portraying mothers with their babies and young children. It would make a one-of-a-kind keepsake for the grandmother-to-be. Mary hoped that would allow Brooke to bask in the limelight when she opened her own gifts.

Mary opened the bookshop on Saturday morning. She had told Rebecca to take the morning off to spend with her family. Business had been slow enough that Mary was confident she could handle it alone for a few hours. In fact, she had time to engage in an e-mail chat with her cousin Jean. She learned that Jean had sold part of her inheritance—Uncle Lew's car—after determining that her son had no use for it.

She had almost forgotten Brooke's promise, but when she checked her e-mail, she also found a note from Brooke and instructions for accessing the art sites she had mentioned. Mary flagged the message and put it in a special file, where she wouldn't lose it.

When Rebecca arrived at noon, Mary went home to eat lunch with Betty. She'd had only half a dozen customers in the morning and sold only a few books. After lunch, she headed off to Dorothy's house and her baby-shower committee meeting.

The other committee members were all business that day, and their plans progressed. Dorothy had found a store in Sandwich where she could get some inexpensive art supplies to use as decorations.

"I think we should clue Brooke's mother in soon though," Dorothy suggested.

"You don't think she'll spill the beans, do you?" Bernice Foster asked anxiously.

Tricia Miles smiled serenely. "We can impress on Linda the importance of keeping this a surprise."

"Ladies," Mary ventured, "I wonder if we could plan a couple of things for Brooke's mother to do, to sort of draw her into this."

"That's a good idea," Dorothy said, and made a note on the pad before her.

"Yeah," Jill Sanderson said. "If we include her, she'll be more likely to keep the secret from Brooke than if she finds out by accident."

"Let's see…" Dorothy scanned one of her lists. "We've already ordered the cake. I'm getting the decorations. Mary's doing the invitations, and Bernice, you're heading up refreshments."

"Maybe we could put her in charge of the gift table," Tricia suggested.

"Great idea," Jill said. "She can make a list for Brooke, so she'll know where to send her thank-yous."

Dorothy nodded. "And you're doing games, Jill?"

"Yes, I already have a couple of good ones in mind."

"Maybe Linda could help you with that in some small way?"

"I'll make a point of it, whenever you decide to bring her into the group."

The meeting soon adjourned, and Mary went home to pick up Gus before heading back to the store. But as soon as she walked through the door, Betty hurried out from her bedroom.

"Mary! I'm so glad you're here. Elle Weir called while you were gone. She wants to see the rest of Aunt Maude's paintings."

"Oh dear. Of course, she did say she'd like to see them when we met with her." Mary glanced at the clock. "It's too late to make that drive today though."

"Tomorrow's out too," Betty said. "They're predicting snow, and I wouldn't want to go that far and get stranded."

Mary nodded soberly. "We'll just have to put her off until next week. I'll be glad to talk to her again though. What do you think of next Saturday?"

"I think that would be fine," Betty said.

"All right." Mary shooed Gus into his carrier. "I'll call her from the store. We'll take the four paintings to her house so she can see them all together."

FOURTEEN

To Mary's delight, Chief McArthur phoned the bookshop Monday morning.

"I've got the report on that drowning you asked me about. Would you like to come over here and talk about it?" he asked.

"I'd love to." Mary surveyed the store, busy for the first time in days. "Can I make it this afternoon? We've got a bit of a rush just now."

"The Monday-morning crowd?" the chief said. "Sure. Come after two. I should be able to see you."

When Mary arrived at the police station, she had to wait a few minutes. She hoped nothing had happened that would keep the chief occupied for too long.

Soon a man emerged from the hallway leading to the inner offices, and the officer at the desk called to her, "You can go in, Mrs. Fisher."

Mary hurried to the chief's door.

"Well, Mary, how are you doing?" Chief McArthur asked cheerfully.

"Fine. And you?"

"Good, good. Come on in."

Mary went to the oak chair opposite his desk and sat down. "Thanks so much for looking into this."

"No problem." He opened a manila folder. "Although it did take a while to locate the complete report on that drowning victim."

"Were the remains ever identified?" Mary asked.

"Yeah, they were." Chief McArthur gazed down at the papers inside the folder. "A couple of months after the body turned up, after the complete autopsy and some legwork by the state police, they put a name to the Jane Doe. They were able to match her to some dental records from over Ellisville way. Nadine Zimmer. Mean anything to you?"

"No." In spite of the grim subject, Mary was glad to have it firmly established that the woman was not Aunt Maude.

The chief turned a couple of sheets of paper and nodded. "Said she'd gone missing, but she lived alone and no one realized it at first. Back then, communication between departments wasn't what it is now."

"I understand," Mary said. "I really appreciate this. I'm just surprised so many people here still seem to think it was Maude Nelson's body."

Chief McArthur shrugged. "I'm afraid that's how it goes sometimes. The true identification wasn't as well publicized locally as the initial discovery. The body turning up—well, that was a sensation, and several residents saw it, so it made a big impression. This official word came quite a while later, and there were no visual aids, so to speak."

"I didn't even find anything in the local newspaper. I guess the Ivy Bay folks either didn't hear about it or have hazy memories, and the dull explanation was forgotten." Mary leaned forward. "Could you please give me the date of that report?"

"November 19, 1950."

"And the body washed ashore in late August." Mary shook her head. "I still find it odd that Uncle Lew held a memorial service three weeks after the body was found, long before it was positively identified."

"You're thinking he knew something."

"Either that or he was in serious denial. I also haven't found any news stories about Aunt Maude disappearing. Why hadn't he reported her as a missing person?"

"I'm as baffled by that as you are. I checked all the databases I could access, and I didn't find any record of him ever filing a missing persons report. But you know, you could ask the Provincetown police."

"That's true," Mary said. "I suppose if he filed a report, it would have been in Provincetown."

"Yup. If that's where she disappeared from, that's where he should have reported it."

"I still think he believed she left voluntarily, but I will check with the police over there."

"What do you think really happened?" Chief McArthur asked.

"I don't know. Right now, I'm leaning toward Aunt Maude leaving him of her own free will, and Uncle Lew finding it easier to declare her dead than to face the fact that she left him."

"You said he'd served in the war."

"Yes, active duty."

Chief McArthur's eyebrows drew together. "You could check on his military and medical records. Maybe he came home with a load of stress."

"PTSD? That's a possibility I hadn't thought of. It would explain the bouts of temper I've heard about and his inability to deal with her leaving him. Thanks, Chief." Mary picked up her purse and stood. "You've been very helpful."

She went back to the bookshop to be greeted effusively by Ashley.

"Mrs. Fisher! Guess what?" Ashley threw her arms around Mary's middle and gave her a big hug.

"I have no idea what to guess," Mary said, returning her embrace, "but I'm glad you got to come here today."

"Me too. Mom and I sold twenty-seven books while you were gone!"

Rebecca walked toward them, holding a finger to her lips. "Ashley, not so loud. We still have customers."

Mary glanced around and saw Jill Sanderson browsing the British mystery shelves and smiling.

"It sounds to me as though you've had a very busy afternoon."

"We did," Ashley said. "The package man came too."

"Yes." Rebecca nodded toward the back room. "We got a carton of books you ordered last week."

"Great." Mary spotted Gus lying on the sunny window seat, and said to Ashley, "Did you have time to play with Gus yet?"

"Only a little." Ashley darted to the window and stroked Gus's head. In winter, his long gray fur grew so lush that he looked twice the size he did in summer.

Rebecca laughed. "She's quite a handful, but she helped one mother pick out half a dozen books for her children."

"That's a big sale," Mary murmured. "Ashley is an asset, the way I see it, and she always perks up my day."

She went to the back room to leave her coat and then settled down at the counter. Jill brought a spy novel to the checkout, and Mary rang it up for her and chatted for a few minutes. When Jill had left, she turned to her computer and looked up a nonemergency telephone number for the Provincetown Police Department.

"It will take time to pull those records, ma'am," the desk sergeant told her. "Besides, I can't just give out all kinds of information over the phone. If you came in here and showed some ID, then I could maybe tell you a few things. You say you're Mr. Nelson's next of kin?"

"Yes," Mary said. "My sister and I are his heirs. He didn't have any children."

"I see. Well...could you come in tomorrow around ten?"

Mary thought quickly. "Yes, I think I could. Would it help if Chief McArthur vouched for me?"

"No need for that. I'll see what I can locate for you."

Mary thanked him and hung up. She called Rebecca over and arranged for her to open the store the next morning. With that taken care of, Mary opened an inventory file to see what books she needed to reorder.

When she got home that evening, Betty handed her several envelopes that had come in the mail. Among them were handmade valentine cards from her daughter Lizzie's children, Emma and Luke.

"Aren't they sweet?" Betty asked. "I got some from Betsy and Allison." She brought her cards over to show Mary.

The handcrafted tokens inspired Mary. She could make cards for Ashley and Henry, along with some cookies. After supper, she spent some time creating the cards. When they were finished to her satisfaction, she also made some for Betty and Rebecca. She had already mailed her store-bought cards to her children and grandchildren.

She put away her supplies when she was done and sat down at the computer. If she wanted to make the album she'd thought of for Brooke's mother, she'd better get started on that. The shower was only a couple of weeks away.

A great many artists had painted Madonnas with the Christ child, and she chose a few of those she especially liked. Then she studied the works of other artists who painted mothers holding young children. She found one by Mary Cassatt that she felt would make a good cover image and copied it.

When she had found a dozen images for her album, Mary decided to use the sites Brooke had told her about to look for Maude Nelson as a painter. She found nothing and expanded her search to include Maude Price and Maude Price Nelson. But her efforts were fruitless. Her only conclusion was that Maude had not produced an abundance of paintings, and none had been sold recently.

The next morning, the good weather held, and Mary set out for Provincetown. Betty had declined to go with her, because she and her sister-in-law, Eleanor Blakely, had arranged to go shopping together. As she drove down the Cape, Mary noted the landscape was much snowier than it had been when she and Betty went out to sort Uncle Lew's things. Even in its stark winter bareness, she saw beauty everywhere she looked.

As she rounded a curve, a stretch of rocky shore struck her as the perfect inspiration for her next painting. She stopped the car and got out, walking slowly along the edge of the road for the ideal shot. The snow beyond the plow's ridge was only a couple of inches deep, and she wandered about for a few minutes, snapping views of the bay and the barnacle-covered rocks. She even got a picture of a hardy bird stalking along near the waterline.

She arrived at the police station right on time and walked confidently up to the front desk.

"I'm Mary Fisher, and I have an appointment." She held out her driver's license.

The sergeant smiled. "You sure do. I'm Sergeant Riddle. We spoke on the phone. Come right this way, Mrs. Fisher."

He came from behind the desk, leaving a civilian secretary in charge, and took Mary down a hallway and into a room that held a row of file cabinets, two oak tables, several chairs, and a wall of lockers.

"This is our duty room, ma'am." He led her to one of the tables. "Have a seat."

Mary sat next to him and set her purse on the floor. "I appreciate your finding this information for me."

"Well, since Mr. Nelson is deceased and you're his next of kin, the chief said it was okay to tell you the basics of the case. See, Lewis Nelson was the subject of an investigation in late 1950."

Mary's throat went dry. Could it be true? Uncle Lew had been suspected of killing Aunt Maude?

"Can you tell me why?"

"Well, that's tricky. I can't let you see the police report, but there's a fellow who knows more about it than I do, and he can probably help you out. One of the officers who investigated your uncle—he was a detective at the time—is still living here in Provincetown. He's retired, of course, but his memory's pretty good. I gave him a call yesterday afternoon, and he said he'd be willing to discuss the case with you."

"That's very kind of him," Mary said.

The sergeant gave her a card with the man's name and address on it, and Mary drove there in a matter of minutes. She parked in the driveway of the small brick ranch house and walked up to the front door. When she rang the bell, a tall, white-haired man with glasses opened the door.

"Detective Lane?" Mary asked.

He laughed. "Long retired, ma'am. You can call me Rick."

"I'm Mary Fisher."

"Come in, Mrs. Fisher. I've been expecting you. My wife has a pot of coffee going, if you'd like some."

"That sounds good, thank you."

She followed him into a snug, sunny kitchen, where Rick introduced her to his wife, Julia.

"I'll get your coffee and leave you alone," Julia said. "I know sometimes these old cases can be distressing, and you don't need an audience."

"I don't mind," Mary said. "These events happened when I was only an infant."

She and Rick sat down at the maple table, and Julia left them with mugs of coffee and a plate of sugar cookies.

"So, you remember the case," Mary said tentatively.

Rick stirred a spoonful of sugar into his coffee. "I sure do. Mrs. Nelson disappeared, and her husband held a funeral for her. Then we got word that the body they'd thought was hers wasn't hers at all."

"That's what Chief McArthur in Ivy Bay told me."

Rick nodded. "Well, that's when we started to wonder what really happened to Mrs. Nelson. Her husband didn't seem too worried about her anymore. He'd supposedly buried her, but they didn't have a body to bury. And when we informed him that the body the medical examiner had performed the autopsy on wasn't Mrs. Nelson, he didn't seem very upset. I asked him if he wanted to file a missing persons report, and he sort of shrugged it off."

"Why do you think that was?" Mary asked.

"Well, he said he'd decided she up and left him of her own accord, and he didn't want to pursue it."

"But you did."

"Sure I did." Rick sipped his coffee, then smiled at her. "I was a hotshot detective back then, and it was one of my first cases. I was just sure he'd done her in."

Mary studied his face and noted the twinkle in his eyes. "But you're smiling now."

"Oh yes. The joke was on me."

"How do you mean?"

Rick laughed. "Roughly six weeks later, the chief told me to close the case."

"Why would he do that?"

"Because we got proof that Maude Nelson was still alive."

Mary's jaw dropped. "I…don't suppose you can share with me what that proof was."

"I don't see why not. The chief had received a letter from Maude Nelson, stating that she was alive and well and had left Provincetown of her own free will. And enclosed in the letter was a photograph of her holding up a *Boston Herald* from a couple of days before. She said she didn't want to disclose where she was and didn't want any contact with Mr. Nelson, but she wanted it in the record that there hadn't been any foul play." Rick picked up a cookie and dunked one edge of it in his mug. "I figure she'd heard about all the speculation, wherever she was, and wanted to stop it cold."

Mary thought that over while Rick ate his cookie. "I think I'm relieved."

He chuckled. "You should be, if you thought your uncle killed your aunt."

"My great-uncle and great-aunt, but yes, of course you're right. It *is* a relief. I just…didn't expect it to all be explained so suddenly. And there's no way that letter and picture could have been faked?"

"I'm pretty sure there wasn't—not back then. Nowadays I'd wonder, but we all agreed at the time it was legit. Do you have any reason to think it was bogus?"

"Oh no. None at all. Where was the letter mailed, if I may ask?"

"Boston."

"Did she look well in the picture?"

"As I recall, she did. Smiling and everything. And at the bottom of the letter, she'd written, *Happy New Year, Officers*. It was only a few days into January when we got it."

"Wow. That means Aunt Maude lived at least four months after the memorial service."

"I'd take that to the bank."

Mary nodded. The evidence pointed toward Maude having disappeared voluntarily and living for some time afterward in another location, perhaps under another name. Her own investigation wasn't done yet. Mary still wanted to know where Aunt Maude had gone.

And if, as the picnic painting suggested, she'd become a mother, what had become of that child?

FIFTEEN

◆◆

Mary spent a good hour examining Maude's paintings at the house Tuesday evening. In a few days, she and Betty would wrap them and take them to Elle, and she wanted to make sure she had noticed anything pertinent.

Again, she picked out the redheaded man in each scene. She believed he was a real person. Perhaps when she saw all the paintings together, Elle could tell them who he was.

The redheaded figure in the beach scene caught her eye. He walked away from her, down the beach, with the dog trotting at his side. Mary hadn't been able to find anyone who remembered an Irish setter around town that long ago. She looked back and forth between the paintings, studying the man's jeans, his shirts, his hair so far as she could see it, and his floppy hat.

She caught her breath as she stared at the hat on the beach-scene figure. The swirl created by the hat's crown almost looked like—no, it *did* look like—one of cryptic symbols Maude and Elle used in their notes to each other.

Mary ran to her desk and grabbed the notebook in which she had listed all the different symbols and the meaning of those she had decoded. She took it back to the guest room and compared the drawings on her list to the subtle lines painted on the man's hat in the beach picture. The symbol it resembled was one for which she hadn't discovered the meaning.

She moved along the wall from one framed painting to the next, examining the man's hat carefully in each one. Sure enough, she could make out a code symbol on his hat—but a different symbol on each one. Her heart beat faster. Together, would they form a message? One that Maude had thought only Elle could understand?

She sketched out the four symbols. One of them she was sure she knew. It was the one Maude had drawn beneath Elle's name on the sticky note directing the painting to her, the one that signified the letter *L*. Were there others hidden in the paintings that she had missed?

Elle's painting, she thought. She went to her computer and brought up the photos she had taken of the paintings. She opened the one of Elle's village scene and located the figure of the red-haired man.

How could she have missed that before? The symbol on his hat was so clear that it showed up even in the photograph on her screen. It was the girls' substitute for the letter *M*, which Maude had used to sign all her notes to Elle.

She went back to the others and tried to make each symbol match up with one of those on her list from the notes and letters. Only one of them could be tentatively matched—the one standing for the letter *O*.

Mary was encouraged. She knew some of the girls' symbols stood for entire words, but she had found three she could give meaning to in the paintings, and each one represented a single letter. Perhaps if she could learn what the other two stood for, she could make out the message. She was now firmly convinced that it *was* a message. Unfortunately, her key included only twelve of the twenty-six letters of the alphabet. More than ever, she wanted to talk to Elle and get her opinion when she saw all the paintings together.

Her discoveries prompted Mary to spend some time trying to come up with words containing the letters *L*, *M*, and *O*. She came up with several five-letter words, and scribbled them in her notebook. Moral? Lemon? Moles? Motel? But who could say that the message contained only five letters? Perhaps there were other clues she'd missed—or other paintings she and Betty had not received.

She spent the next two hours doing online research about codes and ciphers, but couldn't find anything to explain the particular symbols Maude and Elle had used. They didn't seem to go together, but rather appeared to be a mishmash of doodles. She supposed that was what schoolgirls would do.

"Mary?"

She turned toward the open doorway and answered Betty's call. "I'm up here."

"I'm making tea. Want some?"

"I'll be right there." She stood and stretched the kinks out of her neck and back. Saturday was only four days away. If she was right, Elle Weir would be able to answer some of her questions then.

———

The next morning, Henry Woodrow entered the bookshop only minutes after Mary unlocked the door.

"Good morning." Mary smiled at her friend. She had hoped she would see him today—Valentine's Day had come, and she had yet to deliver her card to him, though she'd given Rebecca hers and Ashley's the day before, with a container of cookies.

Henry walked over to the counter and laid a pink envelope down in front of her. "Just making a delivery."

"For me? Thank you! Actually, I have one for you too." She bent down and took the card she had made from the shelf beneath the counter and handed it to him. "Happy Valentine's Day, Henry."

They both opened their cards and stood reading them in silence for a moment. Henry's card was beautiful—obviously a top-of-the-line greeting from a gift shop. Inside, below the printed verse were the handwritten words, "Mary, I'm so glad you moved to Ivy Bay. Here's to the good times. Henry."

He looked up, a smile curving his lips. "Looks like you put some time into making this. Thank you."

"It's not much."

"Sure it is." Henry tucked it carefully into the pocket of his parka.

"Oh, and I made you these too." She took out the small container of cookies she had saved for him.

"Wow! Thanks. Have you found out any more about your great-aunt?"

"A few things." Mary leaned on the counter and told Henry the latest details she'd learned about Aunt Maude's disappearance.

"So you were right," he said when she'd related her conversation with retired detective Rick Lane. "You thought there was something odd about that memorial service all along."

"Yes—but even if she didn't die then, I still want to know the real story."

"You mean, why she left? Isn't it obvious? She told her friend her husband hit her, and she was going away with someone else."

"But that isn't the end of the story," Mary insisted. "I want to know where they went and what sort of life Aunt Maude had after that. And if she had children, and if she kept painting, and—oh, a thousand things!"

Henry's brow furrowed. "I guess I wouldn't expect otherwise from you. You always want to get to the bottom of things."

Mary sighed. "I suppose I should be satisfied with what we've found."

"No, I wouldn't say that. There's obviously more to this, and you're inquisitive enough that it will bother you for the rest of your life if you don't find out the truth."

"That's it," Mary said. "I find it impossible to walk away from a question."

Henry smiled. "Let me know if I can help."

The door opened, and three of the women from Mary's prayer group came in, laughing together.

"See you later." Henry picked up his box of cookies, turned toward the door, and greeted the ladies on his way out.

Mary went to the next painting workshop armed with her photos of the shore on the way to Provincetown. Brooke's lesson on perspective, and her tips on special brush techniques, inspired Mary to clip a sheet of palette paper to her easel and let loose. Roughing out the jagged rocks gave her the same thrill she experienced when she created a new ice-cream flavor that tickled the taste buds. She added a suggestion of bedraggled seaweed on the strip of sand between the gentle waves and the thin layer of snow above the waterline.

"Mary, how wonderful!"

She looked up to find Brooke looking over her shoulder.

"Thank you! I snapped some pictures the other day when I drove out to the Cape."

"It's very passionate. I believe you've found your inner artist."

Mary laughed. "I like that." She tilted her head and eyed her scene critically. "You know, I wanted to add a bird over here, but I wasn't quite sure where to put it, and now it may be too late."

"Too late?" Brooke asked. "It's never too late. Artists go back and add things to their paintings all the time."

"Really?"

"Sure. Even after they've been finished for years. There are some famous paintings that have figures added later on."

"Wow. Can you show me how to put the bird in without messing up the rock, then? I was thinking I'd put a sandpiper there."

"Easy. Now, if you were using oils, you'd have to wait until it dried, but since you're using acrylics tonight, it's no problem."

Brooke opened her own tablet of palette paper and took Mary's brush. In seconds, she had created a simple but convincingly realistic sandpiper on her paper. Mary stared at it.

"Wow. You make it look so easy."

"It's not hard. You try it here first and then on your picture. Put the feet and legs down first, because you'll need to make sure you place it exactly where you want it on the rock. You don't want to plop its body down and then realize its feet will hang over the edge."

Mary worked at it on the tablet, and her bird, though not as animated as Brooke's, was definitely a sandpiper.

"Great job," Brooke said. "Now put him on the rock."

"Okay, here goes." Mary held her breath and used a fine brush to sketch in a suggestion of the sandpiper's feet. From the distance of the viewer, they wouldn't show up distinctly, so she didn't make the detail too fine. Next came the body, and finally the head.

"Fantastic," Brooke said. "Now shade his feathers a little and give him an eye and a beak."

"Thanks," Mary said. "It's not too bad, is it?"

"Not at all."

Brooke patted her shoulder and moved on to see what Betty was doing. In Mary's opinion, her sister's view of their back garden in winter was much better executed than her seascape. Betty seemed to have a flair for capturing detail.

At the end of the class, Mary put her things away and chatted for a few minutes with one of the other students. When she walked over to the refreshment table to get a cup of tea, Linda greeted her warmly.

"Mary! Having a good time?"

"Oh yes, these classes are incredible! Brooke is such a wonderful teacher." Mary fixed her cup of tea as she spoke. "How are things at your house, Linda?"

"Great! I'm decorating the nursery."

Mary looked up at her. "The nursery? At your house?"

Linda laughed. "Yes, isn't it fun? When Brooke came along, we were poor as church mice, and I couldn't do much. But now I can, and I'm turning the guest room into a guest nursery, for when I get to have the baby over."

"Oh, I see." Mary wondered where the adult guests would sleep now, but she didn't ask.

"And I'm doing it all in a teddy-bear motif. Brooke's using Noah's ark at her house, so I wanted to be different. But you should see it! In fact, I'll have to invite everybody over when we're done. It is so cute, you won't believe it until you see it. I found the perfect curtains."

Linda gushed on, and Mary sneaked a look across the room, where Brooke was standing with a couple of other women. The pained expression on Brooke's face told Mary she had heard every word. She turned back to Linda and, as soon as she stopped talking long enough to take a breath, said, "That sounds adorable. So, are you thinking about your garden yet?"

On the way home from the class, Mary couldn't help but ask Betty, "Don't you think Linda is going overboard, even for a first-time grandmother?"

"Well, yes. I do feel a little sorry for Brooke. Maybe her younger sister will get married and have a few kids too, and then Grandma can spread the love around. In the meantime, I'm afraid Brooke will have to grin and bear it."

Mary shook her head. "I know having her mother close by is much better than not having her around at all, but still... I do hope Linda doesn't spoil that child as badly as she says she will."

On Friday morning, two of the painting-class students stopped by the bookshop, and several other customers came in as well. Mary and Rebecca enjoyed the morning thoroughly as they helped the shoppers find just the right books and chatted with them about authors in the mystery genre.

Shortly before noon, Virginia Livingston entered, and she strode directly to the counter. Mary bustled over and smiled at her.

"Hello, Virginia. May I help you?"

"Mary, hello. I came to tell you about something I saw yesterday in Barnstable."

"Oh?"

Virginia nodded firmly. "I happened by a gallery and decided to go in and browse. I couldn't believe my eyes."

Mary's pulse quickened. "What was it?"

"A painting so much like my Maude Nelson—oh, not exactly like it, but the same style, and I don't think it was Ivy Bay. It's a village street, with water in the background. The buildings look quite distinctive, but I didn't recognize them. You can see the steeple of a church and a couple of stone edifices."

"Really!" Mary reached for her notepad. "Do you think it could be Provincetown?"

"I don't think so, but you might know better than I would."

"Can you give me the name of the gallery?" Mary asked.

"Certainly. It was Wave Crest." She gave Mary the location. "Another thing—I'm not sure it's your aunt's work, though it looked so much like hers. It was signed with initials only."

"Not Aunt Maude's?"

"No. I can't remember exactly what they were." Virginia pursed her lips and shook her head. "I should have written it down. *R*-something, I think."

"All right. Thank you. I'll try to get over there to see it if I can."

"No problem." Virginia sighed and looked around. "Well, since I'm here, have you got a nice murder mystery for me? I need something distracting."

Mary chuckled. "I think we can fill that request. Come right this way."

———

Betty came to the bookshop and picked up Mary at two that afternoon. Mary had left Gus at home after lunch and arranged with Betty to drive together to Barnstable, leaving Rebecca to close up the shop.

They found the Wave Crest Gallery without much trouble, and Betty parked outside. The business was located in a busy part of town, and Mary guessed they got a lot of traffic in summer.

Inside, the gallery looked and felt prosperous. The thick carpet and designer lighting to show off each work of art made it seem almost like a museum.

A woman in a gray tailored pantsuit with a rose-colored blouse stepped toward them, smiling.

"Good afternoon, ladies. I'm Sandra Williams. Is this your first time in the gallery?"

"Yes," Mary said. "We live in Ivy Bay, and a friend of ours told us she'd seen a painting here that we might like to see. A village scene, maybe from the 1950s."

"*Hmm.*" Sandra frowned for a moment, and then her face cleared. "I think I know the one. Was your friend here yesterday?"

"That's right," Mary said.

"Yes, I remember. She asked me about the artist, but I'm afraid I didn't know much. Let me show you the piece. It's quite charming." Sandra led them into a side room and turned to face the inner wall. "Here's the one she was interested in."

Betty caught her breath. "Oh my. It *does* look like hers."

Mary studied the canvas carefully. She noted that the red-haired man did not appear in the picture, but didn't mention it. "Yes. Same bright colors and whimsical style. It's not Provincetown though."

"I agree." Betty leaned in and peered at the signature. "RML."

"After your friend asked about it, I tried to find out more about the artist," Sandra said. "I haven't learned much yet. I believe the painting is circa 1960, however. It would help if we knew the place."

"That's not Barnstable, is it?" Betty asked.

"No, afraid not. There is a paper backing, and it has the stamp of a frame shop on it. That may be a clue, but I haven't had time to follow up on it."

"Did you write it down?" Mary asked.

"No, but if you'll help me, I'm willing to take the frame down and let you see it."

Mary laid down her purse and helped Sandra lift down the wooden frame. Sandra carried it out to the counter and laid the painting face down on the surface. Mary took a pair of magnifying glasses from her bag and peered at the stamp on the wrapping paper.

"It looks like 'J. A. Knowlton Framers.'"

Betty had a small notebook and pen out. "Got it."

"Thanks." Mary straightened. "I suppose you wonder why we're so avidly interested in this."

Sandra smiled. "As a matter of fact, I do."

"Our great-aunt was a painter from this period, and this piece looks a lot like hers. However, as far as we know, she always signed her pieces 'Maude Nelson.'"

"A local artist?"

"Ivy Bay, and later Provincetown," Mary said.

"I can make a note of it, and if I hear of any Nelson works on the market, I can notify you," Sandra said.

"Thank you." Mary took out one of her business cards and gave it to her. She wanted to snap a photo of the painting with her cell phone, but a conspicuous sign had warned them No Photography as they entered the gallery.

Mary checked the price tag. Five hundred dollars. That seemed a bit steep for an unknown artist, but she supposed that in summertime, if the right tourist became enamored of the painting, he or she might pay that. For a brief moment, she considered buying it herself, but that seemed extravagant when she had no idea who RML was. One of her next tasks would be searching for other paintings by the mysterious artist.

She and Betty went out to the car.

"Home?" Betty asked.

Mary looked at her watch. "You know, I don't think the county clerk's office is closed yet. Would you mind driving by there? If Bea's still working, I'd like to spend a few minutes in the records room."

"You don't waste much time when you're on the trail of a mystery, do you?" Betty smiled and turned toward Ivy Bay.

Mary nodded in satisfaction. "At least not when I have some new clues to investigate."

SIXTEEN

◆◆

M ary loved the county clerk's office. It smelled of old documents and of secrets long kept but waiting to be revealed. Cupboards and file cabinets crowded every inch of Bea Winslow's office, and in the basement were even more files—row upon row of even older records.

"Hello, Mary!" Bea looked up as Mary entered, and smiled. Her eyes twinkled over the top rim of her glasses.

"Hi," Mary said. "I know it's close to closing time, but I have what I hope is a quick question." She took out the slip of paper on which Betty had written the name of the frame shop. "I'm trying to locate a framing shop called J. A. Knowlton Framers. I believe it was located on Cape Cod in the 1960s."

"*Hmm.* It's no longer in existence, I take it?"

"To be honest, I haven't had time to check. I just got this information at an art gallery, and I thought I'd stop here on my way home. Otherwise, I wouldn't be able to ask you until next week."

"Well, let me do a quick search online." Bea clicked away on her computer for a few seconds, then waited, her hands hovering above her keyboard. Though she was nearly seventy years old, Bea Winslow did her job so well that the town's residents hoped she would never retire.

"Well, one reference turned up," she said after a moment, "but it's a mention of the shop, not a current ad or anything like that. But it looks as though it might have been in Yarmouth. Let's take a look at an old Yarmouth directory." She rose and led Mary to a cupboard, which she opened to reveal a large collection of old books and periodicals.

"Yarmouth. Here we go. You take 1960, and I'll take 1970." She handed Mary a paperback booklet and took another for herself.

Bea went back to her desk, and Mary sat down in the only other seat in the room, a chrome straight chair with a vinyl back and seat.

After scanning through her booklet, Bea said, "I don't see anything in this one."

"I think I have it." Mary had found the name Knowlton in the index of her directory and now turned the pages until she found a listing. "This is it. They were in downtown Yarmouth at the time."

Bea glanced at her watch. "It's five o'clock, but you might be able to catch the research librarian in Yarmouth. She might be able to find something for you."

"Thanks." Mary waited while Bea got the phone number for her. She made the call immediately.

"Hold on," the librarian told her. "I think we may have something, but it could take a minute."

Mary sat waiting with her phone to her ear while Bea straightened her work area.

"Hello?" the librarian said.

"Yes," Mary said quickly. "I'm here."

"That shop did operate here in Yarmouth, from 1949 to 1964," the librarian said.

"They closed in '64?" Mary asked.

"Apparently. I found a news brief in our archives about a new gift shop opening in the space that had formerly been the Knowlton frame shop."

"Thank you very much." Mary put her phone away and told Bea of the results.

"That's great," Bea said. "Are you all set?" She stood with her keys in her hand.

"Yes, and thanks for your help. Sorry to keep you late."

"You didn't, really." They went outside together, and Bea locked the door. She looked up and down the street. "Where's your car, Mary?"

"I don't have it. Betty dropped me off and went home to get supper started. I told her I'd walk."

"You'll do no such thing! It's dark, and it's cold tonight."

Mary knew her parka and other warm clothes would keep her snug on the ten-minute walk, but Bea sounded as though she'd be scandalized if she drove off and left Mary on the street, so she walked with Bea to her car and got in. A couple of minutes later, Mary was home. As she opened the door, a delicious aroma wafted from the kitchen.

"Hi, Bets! Smells good in here." She unzipped her parka and walked into the kitchen. Gus hopped down from a chair and came over to rub against her leg.

"It'll be another fifteen minutes," Betty said. "It's chicken casserole."

"Perfect. That gives me time to put my things away."

"Did you find out anything?"

"Yes, I learned where the frame shop was—in Yarmouth. But they closed in 1964, so we can't contact them."

"But that's good in a way," Betty said. "It tells you for certain that the painting was framed in 1964 or earlier. So that painter was a contemporary of Maude's."

"So it would seem."

"Maybe they even knew each other," Betty said.

"You never know. I'm not sure how we can get a line on RML though." Mary carried her tote bag and purse upstairs, mulling that over. If she could find this other artist, she might learn what became of Maude.

Before going back down for supper, she went into the guest room and stood once more before the four paintings. Her gaze was drawn inevitably to the red-haired man in each scene. Was he Maude's champion? She looked closely at the man in the beach scene. He was tiny and far away. A sudden thought occurred to her, and she followed the brushstrokes that formed the uneven sand. Was it possible the figure had been added after the rest of the painting was done, the way she had added the sandpiper to her shore scene?

She leaned in close. It looked as though he'd definitely been painted on top of the sand and rock background, but she would expect that. Had he been added at a later time though? The placement of the other figures on the beach made the scene feel almost crowded, and that of the man seemed a little out of proportion—a bit smaller than he should be, compared to the others.

Was it really the red-haired man from the other paintings? Or was it a boy? The clothing he wore was the same as in the others, and the symbol on his hat seemed to confirm that he was the same person. She held her thumb over him and leaned back as far as she could, trying to see the painting as it would have been without the redhead. *It just might be,* she thought. The painting looked complete without him, and more balanced.

Mary stood back and gazed at the picnic scene. Maybe he'd been added to all of them after the fact.

She went slowly down the stairs, thinking about the possibility. Over their meal, she told Betty what she was thinking.

"What would be the point?" Betty asked.

"I don't know. Maybe he came into her life, and she wanted to put him in those scenes." A sudden thought came to her, and it made more sense. "What if she wanted to add those symbols? She used the man's hat for that, and the fact that he's in all the paintings is a clue to their importance."

"She could have just painted them in the sand or the sky," Betty said doubtfully.

"I think he's a clue," Mary said firmly. "He may even be her mystery man."

"I don't see how we can ever know."

"I'd like to call Brooke and see if she can come look at the paintings tonight." Mary arched her eyebrows. "Would you mind? We're taking them to Elle's tomorrow, and I'd like to get Brooke's opinion first."

"All right. But after you're done, we'd better take them down and wrap them, so we can get an early start tomorrow."

As soon as they were finished eating, Mary called Brooke. To her relief, Brooke agreed to come over almost immediately.

Mary helped Betty load the dishwasher and clean up the kitchen.

She was giving her dishcloth a final rinse when the doorbell rang. She hurried to open it, and Brooke came in smiling.

"Whew, it's cold out there."

"Glad you could come," Mary said. "I hope it's not too bad tomorrow. Betty and I are going to visit a friend in Connecticut."

Brooke unzipped her jacket. "I can't wait to see your aunt's paintings." She gave a little laugh. "To be honest, I was thrilled when you called. My mom has come over every night this week to work on the nursery, and it's getting a little old. I mean, I love my mom, but sometimes I'd just like to kick back and relax with Bill in the evening."

"You should have the chance to do that." Mary didn't want to sound negative, but she truly believed Brooke needed some rest.

"She called right as I was walking out the door." Brooke grimaced. "I let Bill answer the phone, and he told her I had just left to visit a friend, so I took that as my cue to escape. I hope she doesn't think I was rude not to tell her."

"She'll be fine." Mary hung up Brooke's coat. "You know, it might actually help the situation if you tell her honestly that you'd like some time off."

"Tell her not to come? She'd be crushed."

"Not if you're nice about it. Expectant mothers need lots of downtime. You need to rest. I've noticed that your mom seems to be in high gear with the baby preparations."

Brooke nodded, frowning. "I love most of the stuff she does, but sometimes it's just…too much, you know?"

Mary nodded.

"And sometimes when people ask me about the baby, she cuts me off and answers for me. I hate that." Brooke winced. "Oh, I feel guilty just saying that."

"You shouldn't." Mary laid a gentle hand on her sleeve. "This is *your* baby, Brooke. Yours and Bill's. Not Linda's."

"I know. It's just that since Dad died, she's alone a lot of the time, and I don't want to give her anything else to be sad about. That's why I invited her to help out with the art classes."

"That was very nice of you, and she's done a terrific job with the refreshments." Mary led Brooke into the living room. "I still think it would benefit you if you told her you're feeling a little claustrophobic."

"I keep hoping she'll get interested in something else," Brooke admitted, "but the baby—well, that's a pretty powerful grandmother magnet."

Mary chuckled. "Yes, it is. Have a seat, why don't you? The paintings are upstairs, but I'm going to bring them down. Betty and I are taking them to Connecticut tomorrow to show one of Aunt Maude's old friends."

"How fun! Can I help you get them down here?"

Mary glanced pointedly at Brooke's protruding belly. "You absolutely cannot. Just sit down. I'll be back in a minute."

Betty came in from the kitchen. "Hello, Brooke! Would you like some tea?"

"No, thanks," Brooke said. "We just ate. But you have to tell me about this wonderful painting." She stepped closer to the fireplace and gazed up at the Federalist-era portrait hanging there.

Mary headed for the stairs, knowing Betty could happily spend hours discussing the artwork she'd collected.

A few minutes later, Mary had managed to bring down all four frames and align them on the sofa. Brooke sat down in a wing chair opposite and examined them, a smile on her lips.

"I love these! They are so quaint and exuberant."

"That's how they make me feel," Mary said. "Joyful."

Mary pointed out the red-haired man in each painting, and the blonde woman in the sundress, placed in both the beach scene and the picnic.

"Now that looks as though it might have been an afterthought." Brooke pointed to the woman in the picnic scene and laughed. "She looks like me."

"Expecting, you mean?" Mary asked.

"Yeah, don't you think so?"

Mary nodded slowly, and Betty stepped in, frowning. "She does *look* pregnant, but I thought it might be just the dress."

"Well, in that one, she's definitely not." Brooke pointed to the slender figure in the beach scene. "I think it's pretty positive she's pregnant in this picnic scene though."

Mary looked back and forth a few more times. "I have to agree. What do you think, Betty?"

"I guess so, but that dress isn't a maternity dress."

"What do you mean?" Brooke asked.

Mary shrugged. "We found that actual dress in Uncle Lew's attic. It's a sundress, just like the one in the beach picture. We think the blonde woman is a self-portrait of Aunt Maude," Mary confided to Brooke. "That's why we're so curious about the dress. We never knew of her having any children."

"She could have miscarried," Brooke said.

"Yes. People didn't talk about those things much back then." Mary felt sadness welling inside her, just at the thought. "Do you think she'd paint herself pregnant if it was a painful memory though?"

"Possibly."

"And you think that figure was painted in after the painting was finished?" Mary asked.

Brooke nodded, gazing at the picnic painting. "It could have been. That one on the beach scene looks like part of the original painting. Her space is right, and she 'fits.' But this one…See how she's standing right in front of another woman? She's blocking another figure. Maybe the artist planned it that way, or maybe not. I'm just not confident either way."

"How can we tell for sure?" Betty asked.

"You may not be able to. But if you took it to an expert, they might be able to tell you if the yellow paint used on that figure is from the same batch as the yellow on this sign, for instance. If it is, that would be a good indication they were painted about the same time. But it wouldn't be conclusive."

"So you think it's possible it was painted into the scene years after the painting was done," Betty said.

"It's possible," Brooke said.

They all gazed at the figure for a moment.

"So, what does it mean?" Mary asked.

But nobody had an answer.

SEVENTEEN

The drive to Elle's went quickly on Saturday morning. Mary drove, and she discussed the upcoming baby shower with Betty on the way. As they crossed the border to Connecticut, the approaching visit loomed before them. Mary fell silent during the last few miles, wondering if Elle could tell them anything new.

The older woman greeted them like friends and invited them into the living room, where she had set out a tray with coffee and cookies. Betty and Mary each carried in one framed painting, and then Mary went back out for the others.

After Elle had relieved them of their wraps and they'd exchanged pleasantries, Mary told her what she had learned from Detective Lane.

"So she was alive and in hiding all those years," Elle said.

"Keeping a low profile, anyway," Mary agreed.

"Do you think it's possible she's still living now?"

"I just don't know. But you can be sure we'll tell you if we find out for sure, one way or the other. Now, let's show you her other work." Mary began to uncover the paintings.

Elle exclaimed over each one as it was revealed. When Mary had opened the last one, Elle stood before it with tears running down her cheeks.

"What a gift your uncle left you!"

Her words amazed Mary. She hadn't thought of this as a particularly generous action on Uncle Lew's part. Rather, she'd seen it as the work of a man who resented his wife's course and had hidden her art away out of bitterness, not with the intention of saving it for future generations.

"I suppose you're right. I know we're enjoying them. I'll admit, though, I was thinking we were lucky Uncle Lew hadn't destroyed them all."

"But he didn't," Betty said. "We have them now, whether he intended that or not."

Mary nodded slowly, seeing the cache of paintings from a new perspective. "He may have even forgotten they were there, after all these years."

"Mary, did you ever think Maude might have put them there herself, before she left?" Betty asked.

"Not really. I thought she'd left them where Uncle Lew would see them and find the note. I still think she wanted Elle to have her painting right away."

"Yes, that makes sense." Betty sat down and folded her hands.

"Oh my," Elle said, walking along the lineup of paintings again. "Please, you two go ahead and drink that coffee before it cools off. I just want to enjoy these. It's so much to take in all at once!"

Mary sat down in a recliner and let Betty pour a cup of coffee for her. She wanted to give Elle a few minutes to absorb the scenes before she pointed out the special features.

Betty poured her own coffee and selected a cookie off the plate.

A gasp from Elle pulled their attention back to her.

"What is it?" Mary asked.

Elle laughed. "This fellow right here." She pointed to the red-haired man who sat fishing off the rocks in the harbor scene. "He's the one you asked me about in my painting."

"As a matter of fact, he is. Do you notice anything else about him?" Mary asked.

"Should I?"

"It took me a while to see it, but once I'd noticed it in one painting, it became obvious in the others. Pay close attention to his hat."

"They're not the same?"

"Maybe, but the light on them is different, and it has a different effect."

Elle stooped closer to the picnic scene. After a couple of seconds, she caught her breath. "I see. It's one of our code symbols."

"Yes, and I believe there's another on his hat in your painting—a different letter of the alphabet."

"My painting is in my bedroom. Let me bring it out here."

"Can I carry it for you?" Mary asked.

"If you'd like. Thank you."

Mary followed Elle down a short hallway and into a cozy room with a queen bed covered in velvety cushions. A quick glance revealed three full bookcases, as well as two dressers. Maude's village scene hung opposite the bed, over one of the bookshelf units.

Mary took it down carefully and carried it out to where Betty waited.

"There he is in my painting." Elle pointed to the red-haired figure entering a shop on Main Street. "That's an *M* on his hat."

"Yes," Mary said. "It's very interesting. As I mentioned the last time we were here, he appears in all five paintings. And the code symbol on the hat is different in each one."

Elle turned her head and stared at her. "This is very odd."

"We think he's important. Let us help you find all the figures. If you look at them all, you might be able to help us identify him—because I think he must be a real person."

"It would be wonderful if you could tell us who he is," Betty said. "We've been calling him the Mystery Man and the Red-Haired Man."

Elle was looking now at the church scene, her eyes roving over the people gathered outside the building. "Oh, there he is, by the fence. Yes, I believe he's the same man, though his hat shades his face in this one. That's an *R* on his hat."

"An *R*!" Mary stashed that in her memory, with the feeling they were close to breaking Maude's coded message. "This one on the beach probably won't help much." Mary pointed to the tiny figure walking down the beach with the dog.

"*Hmm*, not as recognizable, as you say, and yet..."

"And yet, he's wearing the same outfit," Mary said, "and you can see a bit of red hair."

"Yes. And that's a symbol on his hat?"

"I think it is, but it's so small."

Elle leaned in close. "Oh yes, an *O*."

Mary smiled. "That's what I thought. It's one of the symbols you decoded for me earlier."

"What about the picnic?" Elle stepped to the side, where the community-celebration painting stood propped against an end table.

"Near the dart booth."

"Oh yes! I see him." Elle smiled. "I agree. Same fellow. And I know who he is."

"You do?" Mary glanced at Betty, whose eyes had widened in anticipation. "We were hoping you could help us, but I guess I didn't dare hope you could make a positive identification. Who is he?"

Betty stepped closer, and they waited for Elle's reply.

Elle's gazed flitted from one painting to another for a moment, and she nodded firmly. "It's Norman Liddell, an old school friend of Maude's and mine."

"Norman Liddell," Mary said. "Are you sure?"

"Well . . ." Elle paused and studied the fisherman again. "You can't see his whole face, but it sure looks like him. His hair, his clothes, even the way he's sitting. But this is the beach at Provincetown, isn't it? I assumed these were paintings Maude did after she married and moved out there."

"Yes," Betty said. "Mary has done a lot of research, and we're positive all five of the paintings depict Provincetown."

Elle nodded slowly. "Yes. But Norman lived in Ivy Bay. What's he doing in the Provincetown pictures?"

"We don't know," Mary said.

"Well, the hats prove it." Elle shrugged. "The letters spell out 'Norm L.'"

Quickly, Mary reviewed the symbols. "This must be the *N*, then?" She pointed to the man's hat in the harbor scene.

"That's right."

"What did you say his last name was?" Betty asked.

"Liddell," Elle said promptly.

NL, Mary thought, but she couldn't make a connection to any of the clues she'd amassed, except that his last initial was the same as that of the mysterious artist, RML. She realized she'd hoped to connect the cryptic letters to the unknown artist, but instead, they'd spelled out the redhead's name. "He wasn't a painter, was he?"

"Norman? Heavens, no. He helped his father on the fishing boat. I never knew him to be artistic."

"Well, I don't know anyone by the name of Liddell in Ivy Bay now, do you?" Mary asked her sister.

Betty wrinkled her nose and half closed her eyes. "It seems as if there was a family by that name…I'll have to think about it."

Mary turned to Elle. "So, what became of this Norman Liddell?"

"I don't know." Elle ran a hand through her silvery hair. "I didn't see him much after high school. But his father was a commercial fisherman. It wouldn't surprise me if he followed the same path. He was always out on his father's boat in summer. I suppose the family could be gone now. After all, none of *my* people live in Ivy Bay anymore."

"We also located one more of Maude's paintings," Betty said. "A friend of mine has one in her private collection."

"Is Norman in that one?" Elle asked.

"No," Mary said. "No red-haired man, and no code symbols that I could see. Of course, I might have missed something. But her painting seems to be earlier than these, and it's an Ivy Bay scene."

Elle nodded, eyeing the nearest painting, the one of the crowded beach. "He does seem to be important in these paintings, and I don't especially like the way my thoughts are going."

"Then maybe they're headed the same way mine are," Mary said. "Do you think Norman Liddell could be the man Aunt Maude left Uncle Lew for?"

"I suppose it's possible." Elle walked over to a recliner sat down. "I'll take that coffee now."

Betty poured her a cup and took it to her. "Any cream or sugar, Mrs. Weir?"

"No, thanks." Elle took a long sip and swallowed. "Well. I never would have thought it. Amazing, really, that I didn't, but she never gave me a hint. I assumed it was someone she'd met in Provincetown."

"What sort of fellow was he?" Betty asked, resuming her seat.

"He was—Oh, I don't know. He was likable enough, but when I knew him, he was a kid. I never would have thought Maude would fall in love with him. He seemed immature when we were in high school. But I suppose all boys do."

"Yes, this would have been several years later," Mary said. "You graduated in 1941, and Maude and Lew married in 1943. A lot happened in their marriage. What if she reconnected with Norman Liddell, say around seven or eight years after graduation?"

"I suppose it could be," Elle said grudgingly. "He might have grown up, and someone from Ivy Bay, someone she'd known all her life, might have seemed like a safe haven. I still don't know why she wouldn't confide in me." She shook her head. "I have to assume she didn't fully trust me."

"That may have come from your urging her not to leave her husband," Betty said. "And perhaps Mr. Liddell was in a position where he'd be hurt if their relationship were revealed."

"He could have been married, you think?" Elle said.

"I believe I can find that out," Mary said. "I'll try, anyway."

"There's another real person in that scene." Elle pointed to the beach painting.

Mary turned her head to look at it. "Which one?"

"It's Maude. In the blue-and-yellow dress."

Betty smiled in satisfaction. "We thought it might be her. We found her dress in the attic of Uncle Lew's house."

"She used to wear it in the summer."

"Look at this one closely." Mary got up and carried the picnic painting over to where Elle sat. "This is Maude too. Same woman, same dress."

Elle looked down at the figure of her friend. "She looks as though she's expecting a baby."

"That's what we thought," Mary said.

"She and Lew didn't have any children." Elle looked up at her, frowning. "Unless…right at the end, before she left. What if she was expecting then?"

"Something to consider," Mary said.

Elle turned her attention back to the painting. "It has to be her though. It's a remarkable likeness—I'd have known her anywhere."

"We think Maude may have painted herself into this scene of the picnic later—quite a while after she painted the rest of the picture. I have a friend who's an artist, and she said it might be a later addition. But the one on the beach—we think Maude was part of that scene originally."

"But she's not pregnant in that one," Elle said.

"Exactly." Mary shrugged. "And the sundress wasn't a maternity dress."

"You think she painted it so people would recognize her?"

"We don't know. What do you think?"

Elle sat still for a moment, gazing at the figures of Maude in the two paintings. "I suppose she may have been pregnant when she disappeared. But if she was, I didn't know anything about it. Or maybe it happened later. No, it couldn't have, could it? Your uncle wouldn't have had the painting in his attic if she'd added to it later on."

Mary took the painting back to its place and sat down in the chair.

"Can I top off your coffee?" Betty asked.

"Thanks." Mary held her cup out.

"Tell us more about this Norman Liddell."

"He was a year older than me—a year ahead of Maude and me in school. He was quite shy. As I said, his family were all fishermen. He was quiet, unobtrusive." Elle sighed. "I never suspected him, but I suppose it's worth looking into."

Mary nodded, her head already spinning with plans for her research.

———

When they got back to Ivy Bay, Mary dropped Betty at the house and drove to the bookshop. They'd stopped for lunch on the way home, and it was now almost three o'clock. She arrived to find Rebecca struggling to wait on customers who needed help and cash out those who had finished their shopping. Ashley, dressed in overalls and a bright-red shirt, was happily overseeing two preschoolers in the children's area, reading them a story while they built a tower with wooden blocks.

Rebecca threw her a grateful look, and Mary jumped into the fray. The store remained busy until closing time. Mary loved every minute of it, even though it meant the mystery would have to wait. Her evening was already planned for her—the shower committee had another meeting scheduled, and this time they had invited Linda Freeman.

Linda drove into Dorothy's driveway right behind Mary and got out of her car.

"Mary! Are you part of this conspiracy?"

Mary laughed and joined her on the walk. "I sure am."

"I was stunned when Jill Sanderson called me and invited me to come to this meeting. Apparently you all have been in cahoots for some time."

"We've got almost everything planned," Mary said. "Tonight we're making favors and addressing invitations. We thought you'd be a good addition to the team."

"I'm thrilled to help," Linda said, giving Dorothy's doorbell a hearty push. "I'm so tickled that you ladies want to do this for my Brooke."

Mary had made a mental promise to be more of a friend to Linda. She hoped they could find some mutual interests that didn't center on the coming baby. The previous Sunday at church, Brooke had seemed stressed by her mother's comments about the baby, and how she would spoil the child. Linda had loudly repeated that she had put in dibs to babysit when Brooke went back to work, but Brooke's silence on the matter had made Mary wonder if that was to her liking.

Linda joined in every aspect of the shower plans with gusto. When she attempted to change the planned centerpiece and table decorations, Dorothy firmly held sway, telling her the materials were already purchased and they would not change anything at this late date.

"Of course not," Linda said. "It was just a thought."

Mary watched with interest but, for the most part, kept quiet. If there was one person in Ivy Bay who could keep Linda on a tether, it was Dorothy Johnson.

As they addressed envelopes, Mary chose a chair beside Linda. She let Linda gush about the baby and the shower for a while.

"Just be careful not to breathe a word about this around Brooke," Mary cautioned.

Linda's eyes widened. "Oh, I won't! My lips are sealed."

Mary chuckled. "That's one I haven't heard for at least forty years." She looked down the table at the other three women. Maybe she could get in a little research tonight, after all. "All you ladies have lived in Ivy Bay longer than I have. Do any of you remember a red-haired man named Norman Liddell?"

"Never heard of him," Jill said.

Tricia Miles also shook her head, but Bernice spoke up.

"Sure, I remember him as a boy. I think his family moved out of town when he was a young man."

"Didn't his father have a fishing boat?" Dorothy asked. "Or was that his uncle?"

"I'm not sure." Bernice paused to slide an invitation into an envelope. "He was kind of a quiet kid."

"I think he used to help on the fishing boat during the summers," Dorothy said.

"Do you know where he is now?" Mary asked.

"No clue," Bernice said with a shrug.

Dorothy shook her head. "He was quite a bit older than me."

"Well, thanks. Maybe I can do some research on his family," Mary said.

"Does this have to do with one of your mysteries?" Dorothy's eyes glinted as she gazed at Mary.

"Just a family thing," Mary said, trying to keep it as vague as possible. "Betty and I are looking up people who knew Uncle Lew way back when."

"Oh, that's right. You're settling his estate." Dorothy's voice filled with sympathy now.

"These are ready for stamps," Bernice said, tapping a stack of envelopes on the table to straighten them.

"Wonderful." Dorothy stood. "I've got decaf coffee perked, and I'll put the kettle on for those who prefer tea. And we have anise logs and Jill's buried-cherry cookies—I can't wait to try those!"

"Let me help you." Linda rose and followed Dorothy into the kitchen. She came back a couple of minutes later with a tray of cups and saucers. "Who wants coffee?"

"I'll take some," Mary said. She passed her final envelope to Bernice to add to the pile in front of her.

As Linda set the cup before her, she said, "Oh, Mary, I've been thinking about that fellow you mentioned—Liddell. My father used to be friendly with one of the Liddells. I think his name was David. Of course, Dad's in a nursing home now, but I'm going to visit him tomorrow afternoon. I'll see if he remembers this Norman boy. On a good day, Dad's memory is pretty sharp."

"Thanks," Mary said. "I'd appreciate it."

Linda shrugged. "No problem. Of course, 'good days' are few and far between for Dad now."

"Why don't you call me Monday if you learn anything?" Mary said. "We could meet at the Tea Shoppe."

Linda's eyebrows shot up. "That sounds like fun. I was planning to do a little shopping downtown on Monday anyway."

It would be worth taking an hour off from the bookshop, Mary thought, even if Linda didn't gain any information about Norman Liddell. They could talk in a relaxed atmosphere, and she might discover some of Linda's other interests.

Even so, Mary couldn't help hoping that Linda would bring her another clue. One more piece that she hoped would fit into the puzzle she was working on.

EIGHTEEN

---◆◆◆---

Mary handled the bookshop alone on Monday morning and went home for lunch with Betty when Rebecca came in at noon.

"Do you know what I keep thinking about?" Betty asked her as they enjoyed their chicken pot pie.

Mary shook her head.

"The baby."

"Maude's baby?"

"Yes."

"So do I. It's wonderful to discover new paintings she did, but there could be a person out there—a cousin—whom we've never met."

"Yes." Betty smiled. "There could be several of them, I suppose. But I do wonder. We've been blessed, Mary, but we have no idea how Maude lived after she left Ivy Bay. If she does have a child—or children—I'd like to know about them. If we do learn what became of Aunt Maude, maybe we can take it a step further and find out about her child."

Mary had to agree that the thought was intriguing.

Soon after she returned to the shop, Linda Freeman called her.

"Mary, I know I said I'd come and have tea with you today, but I wasn't able to get anything out of Dad yesterday. He wasn't at his best."

"I'm so sorry," Mary said. "Don't worry about my question. And we can have tea another time."

She snatched slow moments throughout the afternoon to slip in a little online research. The matter of James Ludwig bothered her. She'd learned from property-tax records that he'd kept the gallery for three years after Maude disappeared. That meant he most likely was not the "mystery man" she left with. Norman Liddell was looking better and better for that role. But Ludwig had to have known Maude's secret—the one she hadn't revealed to even her closest friend. Mary kept on searching for word of James Ludwig after he moved out of Ivy Bay.

She had nearly given up when she gave one last try, expanding her search to art galleries and Ludwig's name. Chances favored the man retiring when he sold out in Ivy Bay, but she held out hope and was rewarded.

"Yes!"

Rebecca, who was perched on one of the ladders rearranging hard-boiled mysteries on a top shelf, looked down at her. "Find something?"

"I sure did. James Ludwig, who used to own the gallery down the street, moved to Maine in 1953 and opened another gallery there, in a coastal town. So he didn't retire after all."

"He's the one who sold your aunt's paintings while she was alive?" Rebecca knew the bare bones of Mary's investigation.

Mary nodded. "And he stayed in the business after he moved. So he couldn't have been too old and decrepit, even though he owned the gallery here for twenty-five years."

"Sure," Rebecca said. "He could have been fifty or so when he made the move."

Mary bit her lower lip. All sorts of thoughts zipped through her mind. Maude had visited James Ludwig's gallery a few months after her disappearance. Had he known where she went when she left Uncle Lew? Did he know how to contact her? Or had she shown up unannounced in his shop?

James Ludwig was one of very few people whom Mary knew had contact with Maude Nelson after she vanished. Detective Rick Lane and the Provincetown police didn't know where she went—only that she was still alive in January of 1951. Did James Ludwig know more than that? He'd been a source of income for Maude. Had she given him her new address?

———

On Tuesday evening, Mary hauled a carton down the stairs and plunked it on the kitchen table. Betty closed the dishwasher and turned to eye the box curiously.

"What do you have there?"

"The last batch of Uncle Lew's papers."

"Do you want my help?"

"Not unless you're dying to dive into musty old receipts and tax bills."

Betty smiled. "Then I'll pass. My book club meets tomorrow, and I still have two chapters to read."

Mary settled in and began to sort the papers from the box into piles. The system had worked for her before. She would put them all back in the box when she was through, in folders this time, so she could find categories quickly if she wanted to view them again later.

Most of the items in this box were old bank statements, utility bills, and the like. She marked folders for them and sorted on. Maybe this one would go quickly. She almost hoped it would. On the other hand, she still hoped to find something relevant to Aunt Maude's disappearance. In more than sixty years, had Uncle Lew truly not found one bit of information about where she had gone?

Two thirds of the way through the box, she pulled out a folded sheet of paper. As she opened it, her pulse accelerated. *Provincetown Police Department*, the letterhead read. It was dated November 1950, and she eagerly skimmed the letter.

Dear Mr. Nelson,

We have just been notified by the Ivy Bay Police Department that the medical examiner's office has positively identified the body that washed ashore near the boat landing there in August. The remains were not those of your wife, but belonged to a Miss Nadine Zimmer, of Ellisville. If you have any questions about this, please contact our department or the Ivy Bay PD.

Mary read it over twice. The letter was signed by the 1950 chief of the Provincetown PD. So Uncle Lew had been officially notified that the body was not Aunt Maude's. But the memorial service had already been held. Maybe most of Maude's friends and family still thought she was dead.

Rick Lane had said he'd asked Uncle Lew if he wanted to file a missing persons report, and he had declined. Later, just after New Year's, the police had received proof that Aunt Maude was alive. Had Uncle Lew kept that quiet too? Was it expedient for him to let everyone else believe she was dead? And while the newspapers had made spotty reports on the drowning victim's identity, they had seemed to forget about Maude. It must have seemed like a nonstory, once the possibility that she was the drowned woman had faded.

But Aunt Maude was still missing when all of this happened. Mary plunged into the box again and sorted every scrap of paper, but she found nothing more that would help. She did find a couple of family letters, but they shed no light on the situation.

What had she hoped for? A paper saying Uncle Lew had filed the missing persons report, after all? Or maybe a check stub written to a private investigator? But Mary found no evidence whatever to suggest Uncle Lew had launched a search for his missing wife. As much as she wished he had searched for her and wanted her to return, nothing pointed that way.

Betty came into the kitchen, and Mary showed her the letter from the police chief and told her the conclusions she had reached.

"I think it was easier for him to go on telling people Maude was dead than to face the fact that she voluntarily left him. Easier, or...in his best interests."

"You don't still think he killed her?"

Betty's evident distress tugged at Mary's heart, and she jumped up to embrace her sister.

"No, no, I didn't mean that. But if Uncle Lew was mean to her and she left him because of that—with this Norman person or some other man—that would be pretty humiliating for a man like Uncle Lew."

"Well, yes, I suppose so."

"I think when he held the memorial service, he really believed she was dead. Later, he learned otherwise, and it was too hard to face. I guess I was hoping he loved her and made some effort to reconcile, but I'm not finding evidence of that." Mary sighed. "Let's have some tea. There's also a letter here from Dad to Uncle Lew. He wrote it about a year after Aunt Maude's disappearance, and he's all sympathetic to his uncle."

"What do you think that means?"

"That Dad and Mom thought she was dead. I don't think Uncle Lew ever told anyone in the family otherwise. As I said, it was easier for him that way." Mary went to the sink and filled the teakettle.

Betty sank into a chair and read through their father's brief letter while Mary made the tea.

"I guess you're right," she said when Mary brought their cups to the table. "Mom and Dad really believed it, and that's why we grew up believing it. Do you think it was just a male ego thing?"

"I don't know," Mary said. "I wondered before if he was hiding a crime. As dark a premise as it is, now I'm wondering if he was just hiding his own embarrassment. Uncle Lew was a proud man, and add to that possible PTSD, and he may have become thoroughly unstable." From everything Mary had learned so far, it certainly appeared that way, as loath as she was to accept it.

"I wish you could have gotten his medical records," Betty said.

"So do I, but I don't think there's any budging on that. And from what I've read, PTSD wasn't even diagnosed as such until 1980. If Uncle Lew suffered from it, that may never have been recognized."

After her tea with Betty, Mary went to her computer. She found an e-mail message from her daughter. Lizzie could always lift her spirits, and after a few minutes of messaging back and forth, Mary felt energized. What was the use of feeling all glum about Uncle Lew, anyway? Just because he hadn't wanted to follow Maude's trail sixty years ago didn't mean Mary couldn't follow it now, however faint it had grown.

She recalled a snatch from one of her favorite Psalms: *I will go in the strength of the Lord God.* She would trust the Lord to help her learn anything that would be helpful to her and Betty.

She signed off with Lizzie and turned her attention to the art world. She opened the Web sites Brooke had sent her, where she could search for information about artists and their works. After some muddling about, Mary's excitement began to build.

The artist who used the RML signature was not as unknown as Mary had thought. Several paintings with those initials in the corner had sold in northern New England from the early 1960s through the 1990s. The earliest ones she could find by RML had sold through James Ludwig's new gallery in Maine.

Mary copied all the information she could find about the elusive painter. She printed out pictures of three RML canvases. All had the same charming style Maude had used. One was from the mid-1980s, and the brushstrokes were broader, more flowing, but it still had the flair she had come to recognize.

She hurried downstairs with the printouts. Betty was reading near the fireplace in the living room.

"Bets, look at these." Mary held out the pictures.

"What are they?"

"They're other paintings by that artist with the initials RML. They were sold in the seventies and eighties—one in a New Hampshire gallery, and two in Maine. I've found descriptions of a dozen more, but these were the only photos I've turned up so far. Look at them."

Betty set her book aside and gazed down at the papers in her hands. She studied each one carefully for several seconds. When she had viewed all three, she looked up at Mary.

"Do you think they're Maude's? That she took a new name and kept painting?"

"Yes!" It felt so good to say it out loud that Mary rushed on. "It's like a pen name. She's the same artist—she has to be. I mean, allow for some growth over time, but those are Maude's paintings. Don't you agree?"

"You're probably right."

"I'm going to call that gallery in Barnstable tomorrow. If they still have the painting we saw Friday, I'm going to have them hold it. I think that one's hers too. I wish I'd bought it when we were there."

"It does seem likely, doesn't it?" Betty said, still looking at one of the paintings, a view of several fishing boats riding at anchor in a small harbor. "I really like this one. Is that what it sold for?"

"Yes, at the bottom."

"Only three hundred dollars," Betty mused.

"But that was thirty or forty years ago."

"The one in Barnstable was priced at five."

"That gallery owner didn't know anything about RML," Mary said.

"Even if she did—would that raise the price? I wonder what a Maude Nelson would bring today."

"We could ask Mason Willoughby."

"He might be too close to it," Betty said. "It's true Maude wasn't well known in her early days, but if we could prove that she's the same artist as this RML, maybe that would increase the value of her paintings. Or maybe not. Personally, I think they're quite good."

"Brooke did too." Mary took the papers from her and compared the prices. "I guess she'll never be in the top tier, but I think you're right—if someone assembled a broad collection of her work…"

"Are you thinking of buying up all the RMLs you can find?" Betty's lips curved upward.

"Well…no, I guess not."

"Still, Mason would be interested in this," Betty said. "He might even like to display the ones we have in a sort of nostalgia show. That would draw some attention to Aunt Maude's work."

"I might consider that," Mary said. "But only with the understanding that we don't want to sell the ones we have."

"Agreed."

"I did find out something interesting about James Ludwig."

"Oh?" Betty looked up at her.

"It appears he was happily married. His wife's name is with his on the deed for their house here in Ivy Bay, and the same woman bought the new home in Maine with him after he left here."

"So it's unlikely that Aunt Maude was romantically involved with him."

"We'd pretty much decided that anyway," Mary said, "but I did wonder earlier. I'm glad it wasn't him."

"Me too. It's time to do some serious digging into Mr. Norman Liddell."

Betty handed the printouts to her. "I wish we'd find out everyone lived happily ever after, but we know that at least one person didn't."

"Right. Uncle Lew."

———

Linda Freeman entered Mary's Mystery Bookshop the next morning and smiled at Mary.

"Hi. I just came from visiting my father."

"How is he doing today?" Mary asked.

"Much better." Linda shook her head slightly. "Sunday was unsettling. He couldn't seem to focus on anything. I'm pretty sure he knew who I was, but other than that, he seemed out of it."

"That's so hard to see in our parents," Mary said.

"I know. We want them to go on healthy and strong forever." Linda smiled. "Anyway, I asked him about the

Liddell family this morning, and he remembered them. I thought you'd want to know."

"Thanks." Mary had been planning to work on that very question today. "I did wonder, but I'd have understood if you didn't pursue it."

"It's all right. Dad remembered Mr. Liddell, but he's passed on now. The one he knew best was Norman's father. But Dad said he hadn't seen Norman for many, many years."

Mary pressed her lips together. "Well, you tried."

"It's not a total washout," Linda continued. "He told me where Norman's brother lives."

"Norman's brother?" Mary could hardly believe it. She took the sheet of memo paper Linda laid on the counter and read the name Jimmy Liddell and an address in nearby Sandwich. "Wow. Thank you so much." This might be a good time to have a private word with Linda about Brooke. Mary looked across the room. Rebecca was talking to the only other customer in the shop. "Would you like to have a cup of tea here, Linda? I've got a kettle out back. We could sit down by the fireplace."

"Sure." Linda unbuttoned her jacket.

"Why don't you browse while I get it," Mary said.

A short time later, they settled in the armchairs at the back of the store.

"That fire feels so good," Linda said. "And it's so cheerful! I love using my fireplace, but I'm not sure I should once the baby comes."

"Well, it will be spring soon, and a lot warmer than it is now," Mary pointed out.

"True. But by the time I begin using it again in the fall, the baby will be crawling. I know I shouldn't worry, but I do. I've been thinking of all the ways I need to baby-proof the house. Yesterday I went through every bathroom and moved all the cleaning products up high so she won't be able to reach them. And I bought some safety plugs for all the electrical outlets."

"That's probably a good idea. Little ones move so fast!" Mary took a sip of her tea and sat back to study Linda's face. "How are you and Brooke getting along lately?"

"Just great." Linda's smile seemed to slip a little. "Well, she's tired, you know. All expectant mothers get a little cranky at times." She chuckled ruefully. "Once or twice lately, she's snapped at me and said I was interfering. But really, I'm just trying to help the kids out."

Mary nodded and did her best to project sympathy. "It's hard to know sometimes when to jump in and when to back off a little. I know my Lizzie loved having me help a lot with her first one, but with the second baby, she wanted to plan everything herself—the layette, the nursery—everything. Oh, she still let me do some things, and I babysat Emma when she went to the hospital, but she was a lot more independent that time. Maybe that's how Brooke feels."

Linda looked down at her teacup. "She did ask me to stop buying everything I saw that had Noah's ark on it."

"She's an artist. She'll know when she's got enough decorations."

"I suppose you're right." Linda sighed. "This is such a huge event. Now that my husband is gone and my younger daughter is in college, I tend to get blue if I'm alone too much. I suppose I may have imposed on Brooke and Bill."

"I'm sure she appreciates your company and your help," Mary said carefully. "It might be a good time to branch out a little though. Find another interest or project to work on when they're busy."

"I saw an ad for a poetry-writing class in the adult education program at the high school."

"You're interested in poetry?"

"I have been since I was a girl. In the old days, I would have signed up. I didn't, though, because it was the same night as Brooke's art class." Linda eyed her doubtfully. "I suppose she could get along without me at the class."

"There's only one more session," Mary said.

"Do you think she minds my being there?" Linda's eyes held a wistfulness Mary hated to crush.

"I'm sure she likes having your support, and you've been very helpful. But if she knew there was something else you'd enjoy, she'd probably prefer that you did it."

"She seems sensitive sometimes when I talk about the baby."

Mary hesitated and shot up a quick prayer for guidance. Before she could speak again, Linda smiled.

"I could bake cookies ahead, and one of the other ladies could start the coffee."

"I'd be glad to do it, if you decide to go to the poetry class."

Linda raised her teacup to her lips. A moment later, she nodded. "Thanks. I'm going to look into that."

NINETEEN

◆◆◆

At the final painting workshop on Friday evening, Brooke came in alone to set up and then sought out Mary.

"I'm glad you're a few minutes early. My mom told me you'd help with the coffee this evening."

"I'd be happy to," Mary said.

"I hope your mom's not ill," Betty said.

"Oh no. She's taking a poetry class, and they're meeting tonight. She asked me if I'd mind—and she went to the trouble of preparing refreshments for us." Brooke laughed and pulled two plastic containers from her tote bag.

"I think that's wonderful," Mary said. "She'll enjoy that."

"Yes, I think so too."

Mary and Betty went into the church kitchen and quickly started the coffee in the big urn and arranged serving platters of Linda's pastries. They set out cups, spoons, creamer and sugar, as well as the fixings for tea.

"Think that's everything?" Mary asked. Most of the other painting students had arrived, and it was time for Brooke to open the session.

"I think so. It doesn't look as nice as when Linda does it." Betty frowned at the table. "I'll bet she usually brought a tablecloth from home, instead of these plain ones."

"Napkins," Mary said. She dashed to find a supply of paper napkins and added them to the refreshment table, then hurried to set up her easel.

The class went smoothly, and no one seemed to miss Linda's presence, though a few inquired about her.

When the refreshment break came, Brooke poured her hot water over a decaf tea bag and smiled at Mary. "Mom said she visited your bookshop yesterday."

"Yes, and she gave me a clue." Quickly, Mary told her about Elle's identification of the red-haired man in the paintings as Norman Liddell. "Your grandfather apparently knew Norman's father, and he told your mom where Norman's younger brother lives. I was able to contact him this morning."

"Fantastic!" Brooke's eyes shone. "Was he able to tell you anything about your aunt Maude?"

"Sadly, no. He claimed he didn't know anything about her. When I asked him about Norman, he was very vague. Apparently, his older brother is still living, but all he would say is, 'He lives a couple of hours away.'"

Brooke frowned as though very put out. "That covers a lot of territory."

"Doesn't it? Millions of people live within two hours of here. But before I could ask for anything more specific, he suddenly had to go, or so he said. I chewed on that all afternoon, and I think he just plain didn't want to talk to me."

"Sounds like it."

Mary nodded. "He definitely knows more than he let on. But I think I'll let it alone for a few days. If I keep trying to call him, he might get upset."

Betty had come up next to Brooke, and now she smiled. "Mary's made great strides in the mystery without his help. She found enough evidence that we both believe Aunt Maude did not die in 1950, but that she left Uncle Lew and continued to paint under a different name."

"Really? That's fascinating."

"Yes, we saw a painting that looked very much like Aunt Maude's, but it was signed 'RML,'" Mary said. "I've found a little more online—and photos of a couple more of RML's paintings. They're not Provincetown or Ivy Bay scenes, but they're very similar in content and feel."

Brooke nodded. "I belong to a couple of online art chat groups. If you'd like, I can ask for information about RML."

"Would you?" Mary squeezed her hand. "You never know where a clue will come from. Thanks."

"No, thank *you*. I have a feeling Mom's decision to take the poetry class had something to do with your talk yesterday. She didn't come right out and say it, but…"

Mary smiled. "Brooke, just be honest with your mom. She's a sweet lady, and she wants to be helpful. She's very excited about the baby—but then, you knew that."

"Oh yes. Couldn't help but know."

"Of course you'll want to let her be a part of things," Mary said. "But I think she's beginning to realize this event should focus on you, not on her."

"Oh, heavens, now I feel selfish."

"Don't. You only have your first baby once. You and Bill should be able to lavish attention on each other and your baby in privacy, as much as you want it. But I know you. You don't want to shut your mother out completely."

"I really don't, although some days I've felt like it," Brooke confessed.

Mary smiled. "It will be all right. But talking to her about your honest feelings will help."

Brooke nodded. "Thanks, Mary."

The next day, Mary came to a decision and phoned Sandra Williams at the Wave Crest Gallery in Barnstable.

"Yes, I still have the painting by RML," Sandra said.

Mary let out her breath. "Fantastic. I've decided I want it. I'll try to come for it later today."

She could hardly contain her excitement. When she called Betty with the news, Betty offered to go with her. Rebecca was happy to man the store alone for the last two hours of business, allowing the sisters to make the trip to Barnstable and be back by suppertime.

When Mary had hung the RML beside Aunt Maude's four paintings in the guest room, she and Betty stood back and surveyed them.

"It *has* to be hers," Betty said. "Look at the water. The waves in this one look almost identical to the ones in our Ivy Bay harbor."

"Maybe an expert could tell if the same person made the brushstrokes," Mary mused.

"Mason Willoughby," Betty said. "Call him and invite him to come look at them."

"Do you think so?"

"It's that or cart them over to his gallery, and frankly, I'm tired of lugging paintings around."

"All right," Mary said.

"Good. I'll start supper. Invite him for dessert."

Mr. Willoughby arrived two hours later. Betty had coffee and apple pie ready, but the gallery owner was eager to see the paintings before settling down to refreshments.

"Yes," he said softly as he peered at the beach scene. "This style is gaining in popularity now. Do you know who taught her?"

Mary looked at Betty. She'd never thought about how Aunt Maude learned to paint.

"We have no idea," Betty said.

Mr. Willoughby continued his study of the paintings.

When he got to the picnic scene, Mary said, "Do you know Brooke Hubbard?"

"Certainly," he replied. "She's a good artist. I sold a painting for her last summer."

"Well, Brooke thought that blonde woman near the table might have been added to the painting a while after it was finished." Mary pointed to the pregnant woman in the sundress.

Mr. Willoughby took a magnifier from his pocket and examined the figure. "*Hmm.* She may be right."

"We think it's a self-portrait of Maude Nelson," Betty said.

He turned and blinked at her. "Indeed?"

"That's right," Mary said, "and she's in this beach painting too." She showed him the figure in the other scene. "Brooke thought she was part of the original composition in this one though. We—that is, Betty and I and Brooke—thought maybe she added the one in the picnic later."

"I see." Mr. Willoughby looked closely at both and shrugged. "It could very well be."

He stepped back to the RML painting and eyed it carefully for half a minute, then took out his magnifier again.

After a few minutes of silence, Mary couldn't stand it any longer.

"Do you think RML is the same person as Maude Nelson?"

"Well..." He turned, frowning. "Not conclusive, of course, but look at the signatures. The *M* in *Maude* seems to me to be very, very like the *M* in *RML*."

Mary and Betty peered at the signatures.

"You're right," Betty said. "I'm convinced."

"The style and subjects are very similar as well." Mr. Willoughby shrugged. "There are people at the Museum of Fine Arts in Boston with more expertise than I have. You might take them there."

"Thank you so much, Mr. Willoughby," Mary said. "We might do that. And if you hear of any more RML paintings on the market, will you let us know?"

"I certainly will. And if you decide to sell any of these, I'd love to represent you."

"Thank you," Betty said. "Now, won't you come have a piece of pie with us?"

"Don't mind if I do."

Mary said, "I'll go get the ledger for you. I think I've found everything pertinent in it, and you may as well take it back."

"Oh, thank you," Mr. Willoughby said. "And I think you've made a good buy on that Nantucket scene."

Mary stopped in her tracks. "Did you say Nantucket?"

"Yes, that harbor scene. The one with the initials."

Mary and Betty both stared at the RML painting.

"Of course," Betty said. "I've only been out there a couple of times, but I should have recognized it."

⸻

Betty was as eager as Mary to continue the hunt, and they went to the county clerk's office together on Monday morning.

Bea Winslow looked up from her desk, her eyes sparkling. "Well, well. I get both Nelson sisters this morning. This must be important!"

Mary laughed. "You might say that. We'd like to know anything you can tell us about the Liddell family."

"Fishermen all. They used to live here in Ivy Bay, but I don't think there's a single Liddell left here now. Let me check." Bea rose and headed toward a row of gray file cabinets.

"We're most interested in Norman Liddell," Betty said.

"Yes," Mary added. "We know his brother lives in Sandwich, but we hope you can tell us where Norman is now."

"Heavens, I don't know if he's even still on this earth," Bea said.

Betty set a foil-wrapped parcel on her desk. "We're hoping he is, and we brought you some cranberry muffins to sweeten the search."

Bea chuckled. "I'd have done it for nothing, but thank you! I had a rather sketchy breakfast this morning, and those sound lovely." She opened a drawer, flipped through folders, pulled one, closed the drawer and opened another.

Mary looked over at her sister and smiled. She had a feeling they were very close to finding out what had become of Aunt Maude.

"*Hmm,*" Bea said at last, turning as she scanned the contents of a folder. "Norman's father sold his property here in mid-seventies. The address he gave at the time was in Rhode Island. Norman doesn't seem to have actually owned any real estate here."

"How can we check Nantucket?" Mary asked.

"I could put in a request to their records clerk. Meanwhile, I do have some old directories." She went to the cabinet from which she had taken the Yarmouth business directories on Mary's earlier visit. She handed each of them a slender booklet. "That's the best I can do for today, I'm afraid."

Mary and Betty quickly flipped through the directories.

"Here," Betty said. "It's from 1960, but there is a fishing cooperative, with Oscar Liddell listed as the owner."

"Oscar?" Bea said. "He wasn't Norman's father. An uncle, maybe?" She went to her computer and clicked away for a few moments. "Here he is." She looked up at them. "I went back in the census records. He's Norman's uncle."

"Would he still be living in Nantucket today?" Mary pulled out the small notebook she always carried with her.

Bea studied her screen. "Doubtful, looking at his age then. But his son Randall...Hold on."

Mary and Betty waited while she did some more looking. "Yes, Randall Liddell has some fishing boats now, based in Nantucket."

"He'd be Norman's cousin?" Mary asked, writing the name down.

"That's right."

The door opened, and a man entered.

"Good morning," Bea called. "I'll be right with you." To Mary, she said, "I'm going to e-mail you this link for the Nantucket Island Chamber of Commerce. You can look it up later, if you want."

"Thanks awfully," Mary said.

"You've been a big help," Betty added. They laid the directories on the counter and left the office.

Betty dropped Mary off at the bookshop, and she used the time before the store's opening to peruse the Web site. The information on Liddell Commercial Fishing was limited, but after copying most of it, Mary followed other paths on the Nantucket site to explore several gorgeous views of the island. One of the photos of the harbor, taken from offshore, made her heart soar. This was the place RML had portrayed in the painting she had just bought.

The night of the baby shower, Mary and Betty went early to the church fellowship hall. Dorothy, Jill, Bernice, and Tricia joined them to decorate the hall and set up the chairs, gift table, and refreshment area. Linda Freeman had been given the critical job of bringing Brooke to the party at precisely the right time. Mary knew no one could do that task better than Linda. At ten to the hour, they all went out and moved their cars to the back of the church or down the street to an empty parking lot.

Wrapped on the gift table was Mary's present to Brooke, a darling summer outfit in size six months—a blue romper with optional snap-over plaid skirt and a fetching, pint-sized beret—along with a teddy bear wearing a smock and beret. Decorating her box was the tiny artist's palette and brush that had come with the teddy bear. Betty had opted for a pewter frame as her present, with a gift certificate to a local photography studio.

Dorothy took charge as the guests began to filter in. Brooke's mother fulfilled her mission admirably, entering the hall at fifteen minutes past the hour with Brooke in tow. The shock on Brooke's face as they all shouted "Surprise!" confirmed that Linda had managed to keep the event a secret.

"Oh! Mom told me she had to pick up something from one of the classrooms." Brooke covered her pink cheeks with her hands. "I was wondering why she insisted I come in with her. I'm so stupid!"

Linda laughed. "I told her going into an empty building alone would creep me out."

"That's not like her at all," Brooke said. "I really should have guessed."

Dorothy led her to the seat of honor, near the gift table, and opened with a couple of games that had them all laughing. Of course, Brooke won the one requiring them to match artists to their paintings, but Lynn Teagarden won the word scramble involving baby-related items.

Next, Dorothy announced it was time for Brooke to open the presents. Linda took the seat next to her daughter, ready to write down each giver's name and the gift.

Betty and a couple of other guests had also wrapped token gifts for Linda. Betty's was half a dozen board books that Linda could enjoy with her little granddaughter. But Mary's album of mother-and-child prints was the conversation piece of the evening. Linda couldn't seem to view it enough times, and during the refreshments, each of the guests took a turn letting her guide them through the pages, each pointing out the paintings they liked best. Meanwhile, Brooke unwrapped each package and exclaimed over the array of gifts for the baby. Linda's preoccupation with the album gave Brooke ample time to visit with the other ladies.

Linda's gift to Brooke was an extra-large box, wrapped in pink paper with bunny rabbits all over it. Her art gift was a large, deluxe set of artist's quality colored pencils, which made Brooke's eyes light up.

"Now, you don't have to save those for the baby," Linda said.

"Oh, but I want to. She won't be ready for them for quite a while, of course, but they'll last. Thanks, Mom."

She opened the big box to disclose a top-of-the-line stroller.

"Wow," Brooke said. "That's fantastic." She leaned over to kiss her mother's cheek.

Bernice called out, "Oh, come on, Linda, tell the truth. You bought that for yourself, didn't you? For when you take your grandbaby for walks."

Linda smiled. "No, that's for Brooke—but I'll gladly use it now and then, if Brooke wants to let me."

"No problem," Brooke said.

As the other women enjoyed their cake and punch, Mary boxed up the art supplies while Linda collected the baby gifts. Mary's carton included finger paints and glossy paper, sidewalk chalk, sculpting clay, fat crayons, and coloring books.

Linda eyed the bounty with delight. "Brooke asked me to keep the art things at my house until the baby's old enough to enjoy them. I can just imagine the good times we're going to have later on."

"I think that's wonderful," Mary said. I know you're going to have many precious hours together."

Brooke caught Mary in the kitchen, as Betty cleaned up the counters and Mary washed the coffee urn.

"I want to thank you, Mary. Not just for the party and the gifts. I...I had a long talk with Mom yesterday, and we both aired some feelings. I think everything's going to be great." She smiled. "Did you notice her attitude tonight?"

"I did. She seemed very respectful, and I believe she truly wanted you to be the one honored tonight."

Brooke nodded. "It was sweet of you to include her. And that album! I told her to let everyone else enjoy it tonight, and I'd go to her house tomorrow and take my time looking at it."

Mary squeezed her hand. "Sounds like a good plan."

Henry sauntered into the bookshop the next morning. He had his hood turned up, but untied it and pushed it back as he walked toward the counter, where Mary sat.

"Cold this morning. It's supposed to be warmer tomorrow though."

"Good," Mary said. "I'm ready for spring."

Henry smiled. "Well, that may be a little optimistic, but the weatherman did say 'unseasonably warm' for tomorrow."

"Hmm." Mary's mind leaped to a new possibility. "I wonder if it would be a good day to ride the ferry."

Henry eyed her keenly. "Ferry?"

"To Nantucket. That's right! I haven't told you." Mary smiled and stepped from behind the counter. "Would you like a cup of tea? I have a tale to tell you."

"You've solved your mystery."

"Not completely, but I think I'm almost there."

Henry's green eyes twinkled. "I can't wait to hear what you've discovered."

He followed her to the back room, where Mary began unfolding her story as she made the tea. When they had ensconced themselves in the armchairs near the fireplace, she concluded, "So you see, I'm pretty sure that Norman Liddell is the man Aunt Maude ran away with, and that they went to Nantucket, where Norman continued fishing with his cousin."

Henry sipped his tea, then sat back and smiled across at her. "I could take you out there in my boat. It might not be as comfortable as the ferry, but it would be fun. Especially since my boat's moored over in Hyannis right now."

"Really?" Mary said. "How did that happen?" The harbor at Hyannis, on the southern side of Cape Cod, would be a much more convenient spot to embark from than Ivy Bay, on the northern shore.

"I was fishing out in the Sound a couple of days ago. I had a good catch and decided to leave the boat over there this week."

"But if you take me to Nantucket, you'll miss a full day of fishing."

"Doesn't matter. It would be a shame to waste that 'unseasonably warm' weather we're getting."

"But it's almost thirty miles out there."

Henry shrugged. "I've done it several times before. We could drive to Hyannis in the morning and get out to the island well before noon. I wouldn't mind. But if you'd rather take the ferry…"

"No, I'd love to go with you, if you really want to."

"Sure. Ask Betty to go along too. And I'll let you bring a thermos of hot tea."

"We'll do better than that," Mary said. "We'll pack a full picnic basket."

TWENTY

Despite the weatherman's prediction, the early morning was chilly, though Mary conceded some might call it warm for February. She dressed in layers, with a thermal shirt next to her skin, over which she pulled on a fleece sweater and a quilted vest. All of this would fit under her down parka, and she would add a knit hat, scarf, and gloves. Corduroy pants and knee socks would keep her legs warm.

Betty also donned her warmest clothing, and she pulled out her wicker picnic basket. After she and Mary had eaten breakfast, she began packing the basket. Mary looked at the thermometer mounted outside the kitchen window.

"It *is* getting warmer. Not quite forty degrees now, but that's still pretty cold for a boat ride. Maybe we should pack both thermos bottles."

"It will get warmer, I think," Betty said, "but you're right. It's going to be chilly on the water. How about one bottle of tea and one of hot soup?"

"Or one of tea and one of coffee. We could refill them before we leave Nantucket."

"Sounds good." Betty filled the vacuum bottles while Mary packed mugs and made sandwiches. They added pickles, tortilla chips, and a small dish of Betty's homemade salsa.

"There. Do you think that's enough?" Betty tucked a zipper bag of oatmeal cookies in on top, with a half dozen napkins.

"There's food in Nantucket if it's not."

"True."

The phone rang, and Betty answered it. Her eyes lit up. "Oh, hi, Linda. That's great! We'll be praying." She hung up and turned to Mary. "Linda Freeman—she called to tell us Brooke has gone to the hospital. It's a little early, but Linda's very excited that her grandchild is coming today."

"I can imagine," Mary said. "She's been looking forward to this for so long." She heard an engine and looked out the front window. Henry's car came to a rest in the driveway. "Henry's here. Are you ready?"

"I think so," Betty said. "I've got my camera."

Mary picked up her tote bag. In it, she carried her notebook, wallet, and phone.

After some discussion, they decided to take Mary's car to Hyannis. She felt it only fair, since Henry had offered the use of his boat, and she didn't want Betty to have to do the driving. The sun did shine a little brighter by the time they reached the harbor, but Mary knew that a warm day on the sea was colder than a lot of cold days on shore.

Henry guided her to the place where he had moored the *Misty Horizon*, and he carried the picnic basket as they walked down to the dock. Because it was off-season, he'd been able to tie up at a dockside slip, so they didn't have to take a smaller boat out to allow them to board.

Betty opted to go right into the snug cabin, but Mary stayed with Henry as he prepared to leave Hyannis.

"In two or three months, this harbor will be packed," he said.

Mary watched him maneuver out past the jetty into open water. She loved the feeling of setting sail, with the ocean and the world before them.

After about twenty minutes, she joined Betty in the cabin below.

"I know I should be out on deck enjoying this," Betty said.

"Oh no. I don't want you getting cold. Let's have some of that tea. I'll take Henry a cup." Mary almost asked if her sister felt seasick, but as she showed no signs of it, decided the best course was not to mention it. The motion of the boat wasn't bad, and she was thankful for the calm seas today.

In less than two hours, they approached the island, and Henry called down to her. Mary joined him in the pilothouse.

"Oh, I see the lighthouse," Mary cried.

"That's Brant Point. It's at the mouth of the harbor. There are two other lighthouses on Nantucket."

"What are those red-and-white things?" Mary peered ahead at the striped items she assumed were navigational aids.

"Those are the range markers," Henry said. "I line up the front and rear markers, and then I know I'm keeping to the channel and we won't run aground."

"How clever!"

"Well, yeah, whoever first thought of them had to be. Those are day markers. At night, they have lights that you can line up."

"How far apart are they?" Mary asked.

"Maybe half a mile. But we're still about three miles out."

"We made good time, didn't we?" She glanced at her watch. "It's just after ten."

"Not half bad for this old boat," Henry said with a smile. "We ran about fifteen knots most of the way. On a nice day like this, I can do that."

He nosed the boat into Nantucket Bay and a place where several fishing boats were moored. "I called ahead on the radio and got permission to tie up here. The harbormaster will send a launch out for us."

Mary went below and found Betty gathering her things in preparation for leaving the boat.

"How are you doing?"

"I'm fine," Betty said. "I was nice and warm in here, and I got several chapters read." She stuffed her book into one of the large side pockets on her coat.

A short time later, they disembarked. It was good to feel the solid earth beneath her feet, Mary thought—and even better to see the charming town of Nantucket.

"I feel silly not to have recognized this place in the painting," Betty said.

"Well, the lighthouse wasn't in that painting," Mary noted. A church tower stuck up conspicuously above most of the old houses and businesses. "I suppose we should have known that tower though."

"Someone should have," Betty agreed.

"Mr. Willoughby knew it right off—and probably Henry would have too. I should have shown it to him first thing."

"Hindsight, dear ladies," Henry said. "Where do you want to go first?"

Mary looked around. "The town office, I think."

He nodded. "I believe the town and county governments are virtually the same here. The building you want is just down there, beyond that café."

Inside the office, they gained permission to look at property maps from the 1950s. While the clerk declined to give out any current information about Nantucket residents, she had no problem showing them the lot on one of the maps indicating property owned by Norman Liddell from 1952 to 2001.

"That property changed hands at the time, but Mr. Liddell owned it for nearly fifty years."

Mary noted the address and asked the clerk for directions. Since it was more than a mile away, Henry went outside to summon a taxi.

"You shouldn't have any trouble getting a cab near the café this time of year," the clerk said.

"I'm surprised they're even running in winter," Betty commented.

"Well, a lot of cabs are mothballed, but we still get a few tourists, and some of the locals use them now and then." The clerk smiled. "We do allow cars now, but a lot of folks out here don't see the need for them, and the fewer automobiles the better in a place like this. It keeps the air cleaner and encourages the nostalgic atmosphere that people expect here.

Mary thanked the clerk, and she and Betty went outside. Henry had already found a taxi, and they all got into the backseat.

As they drove along the street, Betty exclaimed over the architecture of the houses and businesses they passed. "I read that Nantucket has one of the highest concentrations of pre–Civil War buildings in the country."

"I saw that too," Mary said with a smile. "We must have looked at the same Web site last night. And they have the oldest operating windmill in the United States."

"I'd love to see it," Betty murmured. Her husband's family owned a historic gristmill in Ivy Bay, and Mary fully understood her interest.

"There's no reason we can't, if there's time," Mary said.

"It's not far to Mill Hill Park," Henry said. "And the Nantucket Whaling Museum is worth seeing too."

The cab driver made a couple of turns in a residential neighborhood and pulled up before a snug little house on a large lot. Like that of many of the other houses on the island, the siding was of weathered shingles.

Henry asked the cab driver to wait, and they walked up to the door.

"I just love this," Betty said. "And I'll bet they can see the harbor from the upstairs windows."

Mary looked around. The well-kept house was not large, but it had location going for it, and from the look of the two chimneys, she was sure it had some age to it. Nowadays, such a home on Nantucket would probably fetch a million dollars or more. But things were different in 1952. An enterprising young fisherman and a promising artist might have been able to swing it.

A woman of about forty opened the door and eyed the three of them quizzically. Her dark hair was cut short and full, and she wore a green wool sweater and gray slacks. "May I help you?"

"Hello," Mary said with a smile. "I'm Mary Fisher. My sister and I came over from the mainland this morning hoping we could find the house where our great-aunt used to live."

"Oh. And you think this is it?"

"Well, we're hoping. Her name was Maude Nelson."

"*Hmm.* Don't know anyone by that name. When did she live here?"

"We believe from the early 1950s on," Mary said. "This house was owned by a man named Norman Liddell, and—"

"Oh, sure, Mr. Liddell," the woman said. "My husband and I bought the house from him in 2001."

Mary's heart beat faster, and she glanced at Betty. Henry had hung back, at the bottom of the steps, but Betty stood beside her sister, as eager to hear the woman's response as Mary.

"Was he married at the time?" Betty asked, and Mary could have kissed her for coming up with such a brilliant question.

"His wife had just died. That's why he sold the house, which was our good fortune."

"I'm so sorry. She was our Aunt Maude," Mary said quickly. "At least I think so."

The woman frowned. "I thought his wife was named Ruth."

Betty's hopeful expression crumbled. Mary reached for her hand and squeezed it. Everything was falling into place in her mind.

"She was," she said. "That was Aunt Maude's middle name. But after she and Norman moved out here, I believe she started going by Ruth. Ruth Maude Liddell." She said it slowly, and Betty's eyes lit up. Mary knew she had made the connection to the RML artist.

"Well, look, why don't you come in?" The woman opened the door wider. "Maybe we can sort this out, but it's chilly out there, and I don't want to cool the house off."

"Thank you very much," Mary said.

"I'll pay the driver off," Henry told her.

Mary followed her hostess, who led her and Betty into a well-proportioned living room with a fire blazing in a fireplace on the far wall. The antique furniture and old woodwork gleamed in the firelight and the sun streaming through the front windows. Henry soon joined them.

"My name is Adele Hathaway," the woman said.

Mary gave her name again and introduced Betty and Henry. "Thank you so much for giving us a few minutes. We've been trying for weeks to learn what happened to Aunt Maude when she left Ivy Bay, and we believe this is the place—this is where she and Norman came to live."

"Oh. Well, I suppose you'd like to see the house."

"Not if it's any trouble," Betty said. "We ought to have called ahead, but we didn't know exactly which house Mr. Liddell owned until we got here."

"I see," Adele said, but she looked a little confused. "Let me speak to my husband."

She left the room, and Mary could hear distant voices.

"I hope we're not intruding," Betty said.

"Seems like they actually knew Norman," Henry pointed out.

Mary nodded. "Maybe she can give us an idea of where he is now."

"That would probably help more than a house tour, although I love her taste in furnishings." Betty stepped closer to the fireplace and studied the watercolor seascape hanging over it. "I do like this painting too."

Mary walked over beside her and gazed up at the sailboat cutting through the water. "Not Aunt Maude's."

"No. I think the signature says 'Fleming.' I wonder if it's a local artist."

Adele came back into the room with a tall, gray-haired man. His neatly trimmed beard gave him the air of a professor.

He glanced around at the three of them and nodded. "Hello. Adele tells me you're related to the Liddells. I suppose we could show you the lower part of the house, but the upstairs—"

"How very kind of you." Betty stepped forward with a gracious smile and took his hand. "I'm Elizabeth Emerson, from Ivy Bay, and this is my sister, Mary Fisher, and our friend Henry Woodrow."

"How do you do? I'm Donald Hathaway."

When Mary shook his hand, she said, "We're sorry to barge in on you like this, but we do appreciate your hospitality. Betty and I would love to know if you've made any renovations since you bought the place or if it looked just like this when the Liddells lived here."

"Well, ah, let's see." Donald glanced at his wife. "We put in a second bath upstairs, and we did some painting. Kitchen, bathroom, and so on."

"Yes, but it's much the same as it was fifty or sixty years ago," Adele said. "Of course, the furnishings are all ours."

Mary nodded. She doubted Norman and Maude could have afforded the beautiful antiques now in the house.

"Would you like to see my study?" Donald asked. "I'm not sure what they used the room for, but there's a second fireplace in there, and it has some interesting cabinetry. Cypress, I think. Oh, notice the fir floors. Those are original."

"How old is the house?" Henry asked.

"The town records say 1831."

"Fantastic," Betty breathed, taking in all the details as the Hathaways pointed them out.

After touring the study, they went into the kitchen.

"We did have new countertops put in when we moved in," Adele said, "though we kept the old cabinets. Not the most glamorous, but they seemed to fit the house. I believe they're 1960s era. Mr. Liddell may have built them himself."

"Oh yes." Mary nodded with approval at the white-painted wooden cabinets. They did indeed seem an organic part of the modest house.

"We like it," Donald said with a shrug that included the entire dwelling. "I suppose we could live a lot fancier for the same price someplace else, but we love the island life."

Adele smiled and took his arm. "I love to travel, but I love coming home even more. I don't ever want to move again."

"I can see why," Mary said. "Do you know where Mr. Liddell is now?"

"I...uh...believe he's living with his son," Adele said with a glance at her husband.

"That, or his son is in charge of his living arrangements," Donald said. "He's quite elderly, you know."

"Is his son living on the island?" Mary asked.

"Yes, not too far from here, actually," Adele said.

"You might like to see the backyard," Donald said, walking toward the back door. "Adele loves her garden out there. Of course, everything's winter-killed now, but you should see it in June or July."

"There are some plants that your aunt must have planted," Adele added. "Foxglove and hosta and phlox. They come back every year, and I love them. I've added to them, but those were the start of my garden. It was quite overgrown when we moved in."

"We'd love to see it," Betty said.

They all fastened their coats while Adele went to get a wrap.

"I'll let her show you and get back to my reading," Donald said. "It was nice meeting you all."

"Yes, and you," Mary said. Apparently they would leave after seeing the backyard. She determined to ask about Norman's son before they said good-bye.

"Thank you so much." Betty smiled at him.

Henry nodded, and Mary said, "So nice to meet you, Mr. Hathaway."

They all went out the back door from the kitchen. Mary could see that the back patio and garden, though not very big, would be a pleasant place in summer. She could imagine sitting out here and reading, or having tea with friends who dropped in. Only a little snow was visible, in low drifts against the board fence. A large tree dominated the far end of the yard.

"Oh," Betty said. "You have an elm."

Adele smiled. "Yes, we're fortunate. A lot of the old elms died, but quite a few survived the Dutch elm disease infestation, and we have this one."

"Magnificent." Betty strolled toward it, and Mary followed.

"It's very old," Adele continued. "They tell us it may have been planted after the fire of 1846 that killed a lot of the trees. The town helps maintain the trees, even the ones on private property."

"They know how important they are," Mary said.

Adele nodded. "When you get out away from town, you'll see mostly small evergreens and scrub oak—stunted things. But there are some beautiful large trees here in town. There's even a walking-tour pamphlet that guides people around to see the best ones."

They had neared the trunk of the towering elm, and Adele stopped walking.

"There is one thing about the tree. Since you're interested in the house's history, I'll tell you. It was here when we came."

Mary looked at her expectantly.

"You have to come around to the back to see it." Adele walked around behind the large bole of the tree, and they followed. "Here it is."

At about eye level, Adele reached out and touched the gray bark. Mary stared at the scar, long ago healed over.

"An arrow," Henry said. "But what's that? Someone's initials?" He pointed to the mark above the downward pointing arrow.

"We don't know," Adele said.

"I do." A shot of adrenaline coursed through Mary as she gazed at the symbol—the encrypted letter *M* that Maude had used as her signature.

TWENTY-ONE

———— ◆◆ ————

Y ou recognize this?" Adele asked.

Mary nodded. "Betty does too."

Betty cleared her throat. "It's Aunt Maude's name symbol. She and her best friend had a code when they were young, and they continued to use coded words in letters. Mary's been puzzling over them."

Adele smiled. "How wonderful! Your aunt Maude put it there, then."

"I'd say so." Mary reached out and ran her gloved fingertips over the rough bark. "But the arrow..."

"What do you think that means?" Henry asked, watching her keenly.

"Probably the obvious. Something's down there." Mary took a step back and stared down at the ground.

"You mean you think something could be buried here?" Adele asked. "Donald and I have wondered, but we didn't want to dig. We wouldn't want to disturb the tree's roots, and...well, to be frank, I'm not crazy about digging up a pet's remains or anything like that."

"What do you think?" Betty's brow furrowed as she waited for Mary's answer.

"I think she buried something here, for sure."

Adele looked from one to the other of them. "Do you think it would hurt the tree to dig?"

"We could do it very carefully," Henry said.

Mary was thankful that he had spoken up for them, but she had one other concern. "Isn't the ground frozen?"

"We've had mild weather, and under the tree, it's sheltered," Adele said, frowning as though weighing the options. "All right, you've got me curious. Just let me check with Donald. If he says it's all right, then I'll get a spade."

She walked into the house, and Mary realized she had held her breath. She exhaled in a big sigh.

Henry smiled. "Well, girls, if old Donald agrees, I'm willing to do the digging."

"That's sweet of you, Henry." Betty patted his arm. "I'm a bit surprised she's even considering it."

"I hope he won't say no," Mary said. "We're so close!"

"To what though?" Betty's blue eyes were serene, but Mary could sense her underlying excitement.

They didn't have long to wait. Adele came out of the house and walked to a small toolshed at the edge of the yard.

"She's getting the spade," Mary whispered.

Betty nodded. "Donald must have agreed to it."

"Excuse me, ladies." Henry moseyed toward Adele and the shed.

"Yes, Henry, work your charm," Mary said softly.

"I'm extremely glad he's with us," Betty said. "Not just so he can dig, either."

Mary nodded, watching him. "Henry is a good friend to have along on an adventure."

Henry spoke to Adele, and the two came back toward them and the stately elm tree. Henry carried a long-handled spade over his shoulder, with the blade poking up toward the gray sky behind, and Adele brought a small garden trowel and a whisk broom.

"I thought these might come in handy," she said as they approached. "I was in on an archeological dig in my grad-student days, and if we do find something, we'll want to be very careful in how we handle it."

"Good thinking," Mary said.

Henry studied the markings on the tree and positioned the point of the spade's blade a couple of feet out from the trunk, between two large roots that showed for a short ways before they disappeared below the earth.

"About here, do you think?"

"I'd think that's about right," Betty said.

"If there is anything," Adele added.

"True," Mary said. "If Aunt Maude did bury something here when she came, she might have dug it up later, I suppose."

"Or Norman might have before he sold the house and moved away." Betty frowned. "I certainly hope not."

"Me too," Mary said fervently.

Henry stepped on the edge of the spade, and the tip sank into the ground several inches. "Not too bad," he said. "I think we'll be able to do it."

"I shouldn't think it was very deep," Mary said. "Not so close to a tree."

They waited as he carefully set aside the clumps of sod so that he could replace them later. It took him only a few minutes to open a hole roughly eighteen inches square and as deep. Mary wondered how deep they should go. Adele started fidgeting. Would she call a halt to the treasure hunt soon?

As Henry stepped down onto the spade again, a soft crunch sounded. He hastily withdrew the spade. "I'll take that trowel now."

Adele handed it to him. "You think you've found something?"

"Well, I hit something that wasn't a rock." He crouched beside the hole and bent down toward it.

"Let me find a sack or something that you can kneel on." Adele handed Mary the whisk broom and headed for the toolshed.

Mary touched Henry's shoulder. "I heard the noise. What do you think?"

"Not metal. Sounded like wood to me."

"A box?" Betty asked, leaning down and peering into the hole.

"Can't tell yet." Henry's gaze shifted. "Hello."

Mary straightened and looked toward the house. A man had come around the corner and was hurrying across the backyard toward them.

"Who's this?" Betty said softly.

Mary had no answer, but she noted one interesting thing: The tall, broad-shouldered man had flaming red hair.

He strode toward them with long, determined steps. When he was ten yards away, he called out, "What's going on here?"

"Maybe he's from the tree people," Betty whispered.

Mary gulped. She hadn't considered that the town might object to their excavating near the tree.

Henry touched his hand to his forehead in an abbreviated salute. "Morning. We have the homeowner's permission."

The man's green eyes snapped as he looked from one to another of them. He stopped close to them and gazed down at the hole. Mary noted that his red hair had a sprinkling of gray, and his skin crinkled at the corners of his eyes as though he had spent many hours out in the sun. He had to be at least sixty, she thought, but he looked strong. She sent up a quick silent prayer for wisdom.

"Mr. Liddell?" she asked tentatively.

His chin whipped around, and he stared at her. "Who are you?"

"I'm Mary Fisher, and this is my sister, Elizabeth Emerson, and our friend Henry Woodrow. We're from Ivy Bay."

Betty's expression was troubled. "You can't be...Norman."

The man glanced at her, then back at Mary. "I'm Brad, his son. And if you people don't stop digging right now and fill in that hole, I'll call the police."

Adele came from the toolshed carrying a burlap sack. "Bradley?" She walked toward them, frowning. "What's going on?"

Brad turned toward her voice and huffed out a breath. "Donald called and gave me a heads-up. You can't let them dig up Mom's stuff."

Adele looked at him blankly, then glanced at Mary and the others. "I'm sorry, but I don't know what you're talking about."

"My mother's things, that she buried under the tree. You can't let these people have them."

"But..." Adele shook her head. "Your father never said anything about there being something under there. We've seen the carving on the bark, and we've wondered, but he never said one word when we bought the house."

"Well, I'm telling you now," Brad said. "Years ago, my mother put something in the ground there, and she didn't want anyone to disturb it."

"Then why did she mark it?" Henry asked.

Brad glared at him. "That's her business, not yours."

Henry stepped forward and said affably, "I'm Henry Woodrow. I knew your father, Norman, in the old days, back in Ivy Bay."

"You did?" Brad blinked at him. "Were you a friend of his?"

"Not really. He was quite a bit older than me, but I remember when your family still lived in Ivy Bay. Didn't Norman's folks stay there in town?"

"I don't know. For a while, I guess. When Grandpa died, he was living in Rhode Island, but that was a long time ago."

Henry nodded. "We don't want to do any harm here."

"Then what do you want?"

"As a matter of fact, these two ladies are nieces of your mother, Maude."

"My mother's name was Ruth."

Mary spoke up gently. "Wasn't she the artist who signed her paintings RML?"

"Y-yes."

"Would that stand for Ruth Maude Liddell?"

Brad hauled in a deep breath. "You're related?"

"Yes, we are, by marriage."

He studied her face for a few seconds. "How?"

"We're Nelsons."

"So?"

Mary looked at Betty. Her sister cleared her throat and stepped closer to Bradley.

"Mr. Liddell, are you aware that your mother was married before…before she came to Nantucket? Before she married your father, I mean."

"What are you saying?"

Mary's heart plummeted. Bradley seemed to have no knowledge at all of Maude's marriage to Uncle Lew.

Donald Hathaway came out of the house and walked toward them. "Hello, Brad. I'm not sure I understand why you were so upset."

Brad looked at him. "These people…" He looked back at Betty. "They seem to know things about my mom that I didn't know. They say they're related to her. And they want to dig up whatever she buried under the tree."

"And you don't want them to?" Donald asked.

"Well…" He faced Mary and Betty. "I'm sorry I threatened you with the cops. I was upset. I mean…Mom always said that if she wanted to dig that stuff up, she would. But she never did. I asked Dad about it once, after she died, and he said that since she didn't want or need it in her lifetime, we should let it rest. I didn't really think about it when we moved him in with us and he sold the house to the Hathaways. But later, it came to mind. I asked Dad if we should tell Donald and Adele and dig it up. But he said no, like before. Let it rest."

"What do you think it is?" Adele had a look of alarm on her face.

"I have no idea. I always thought it was something from her childhood. I wanted to dig it up. In fact, I almost did once, when I was thirteen or so. But I knew Mom didn't want me to, so in the end, I left it alone." He turned to Betty. "You know something, don't you? Please tell me."

"Mary's the one who has done most of the research," Betty said.

Brad changed his focus to Mary.

"Your mother was born Maude Ruth Price," Mary said. "We knew her as Aunt Maude. That's because she married our uncle, Lewis Nelson, in 1943."

He frowned but nodded. "All right."

"We'd always been told that she died in 1950." Mary looked around to include the Hathaways. "Betty and I think now that our parents truly believed she was dead. But they're no longer living, so we can't ask them. Uncle Lew died a couple of months ago, and we inherited his estate. We found evidence that leads us to believe Maude left Uncle Lew and came here with Norman Liddell."

"That's—" Brad stopped and looked down at the hole. "So, whatever is in there might tell about her old family."

"It might," Mary said. "If you'd like, we'd be happy to have you visit us in Ivy Bay later and see some of your mother's early paintings. I could show you the documentation we've gathered about her early life. And we would love to meet your father. We believe he's in several of her paintings."

"If you don't mind my asking," Betty said timidly, "when did your mother die, exactly?"

"In the spring of 2001," Brad said. "Her heart gave out one day while she was out painting. When she wasn't home by dark, Dad went out looking for her."

"I'm sorry," Betty whispered.

Brad was silent for a moment and then looked up at her. "Did they have kids? Your uncle, I mean..."

"No. Uncle Lew and Aunt Maude didn't have any children."

He exhaled slowly. "I guess we should see what's down there."

———

A half hour later, they all sat in the Hathaways' living room, examining the items from the crumbling oak box Henry had unearthed. Brad studied Maude Nelson's 1948 driver's license intently.

"I guess they didn't have the person's picture on them back then."

"No," Donald said. "That came later."

"I do think we know what this key goes to." Mary took out her key ring and held the key they'd found in the box up against the one she'd received from the lawyer in Provincetown.

"Uncle Lew's house?" Betty asked.

"That's right. She probably didn't mean to carry it away with her, since she never intended to go back. So she buried it with other things that could link her back to her unhappy marriage."

"I don't understand," Brad said. "How could she just dump her driver's license?"

"A lot of people on the island did without cars back then," Adele said. "Especially if they lived in town."

Mary nodded. "And remember, Maude took on a new identity—she used her middle name, Ruth, and your father's last name, Liddell. I don't think she wanted anyone to associate her with Maude Nelson of Ivy Bay."

"But...weren't they married?" Brad swiped a hand across his forehead. "I just can't believe they weren't."

"They may have been," Mary said. "We don't know. Perhaps we could find something in the archives here on Nantucket. But I think it might be easier to ask your father."

Brad let out a deep sigh. "I'll do that. I mean, I always assumed..." He shook his head. "You're right. I'll ask Dad. I just wish there was something like...oh, I don't know, something like her birth certificate, I suppose. And ideally, a marriage certificate for her and Dad."

"She probably needed the birth certificate to obtain other documents," Betty said. "For instance, if she decided to legally change her name, or to divorce Lew and marry your father. But that's another thing you might ask him about. The driver's license, though, was something she felt she no longer needed, and she might have wanted to keep anyone else from seeing it. It has her married name on it—Maude R. Nelson. Her birth certificate didn't, and she'd only switched around her first and middle names, so maybe she didn't think it would matter if someone saw that. It wouldn't connect her to Lew, and that's what was important to her at that time."

Brad frowned and reached for another document from the box. "This statement. It's pretty grim."

"Yes," Mary said. They had all read the bleak handwritten declaration by a neighbor of Maude and Lew Nelson. The woman stated that she had helped Maude on the evening she left her husband and tried to convince her to go to the hospital. Maude had refused. "Do you know what I think?"

Brad looked at her, his eyebrows arched.

"I think she got this statement from the neighbor in case she ever needed to prove to a court that Lew had hurt her. If she'd had more time, she might have taken photos of her injuries. Back then, she may not have thought of it. But she got a signed and dated document from her neighbor, describing the harm Lew had done to her."

"I think you're right," Adele said. "That's what a woman would do if she thought she might need to prove her case someday."

Mary picked up the last item and smiled. "But this letter—this is the happy ending, Brad. This letter tells you that your mother was looking toward a happy future." The letter from Norman could only be called a love letter. In it, he promised Maude that he would take care of her. In the summer of 1950, he had joined his cousin in partnership on a fishing boat, and they were making a success of it. In a few more months, when they had paid off the boat and he had put away enough for them to have housing and meet their basic needs for the winter, he would come for her.

Mary kept quiet about her personal feelings concerning Maude's romance with Norman during her marriage to Lew. She knew Betty and Henry also held back their opinions, out of respect for Brad's feelings about his mother. After all, he hadn't known any of this until today, and they hadn't come to criticize Maude. They only wanted to know what had happened to her, and now Mary was satisfied. She had her answers. Maude had lived on for another fifty-plus years, and she had been happy with Norman and their child, Bradley.

"I think my dad would like to meet you," Brad said, his voice thick with emotion. "He lives with my wife and me now. He'll be ninety-one next month, and it got so he just couldn't live alone anymore. But he still gets around. If you wouldn't mind telling all this again and showing him these things, I'd be happy to take you over to my house and introduce you."

"Did you tell him I'd called you?" Donald asked.

Brad shook his head. "I wasn't sure what it was all about yet, and I didn't want to upset him. But now, I think it might be good for us to talk about all of this."

"And, of course, you'll take him these things from the box," Adele said. "He should have them, if he wants them."

"I'd love to meet him," Mary said.

Betty smiled. "So would I. But it's past one o'clock. Maybe the three of us should stop somewhere for lunch while you go home and explain things to him. We could come by in an hour or so." She sent Henry an inquiring look.

"That would be fine," Henry said. "But we won't want to stay too long. We'll need to get back to Hyannis by dark, if we can."

TWENTY-TWO

＊◆＊

Norman Liddell came out to meet them in the foyer of his son's home. The old man stooped a little, and he wore glasses, but he seemed to Mary a young ninety-one-year-old. Brad introduced him to her, Betty, and Henry, and also presented his wife, Deena, who showed them into the living room. Norman eased down into an old brown leather recliner. Mary and the others found seats, and she looked around the room. The Liddells had modest but comfortable furnishings, and one wall held an array of family photographs.

"So, tell me again how you're related to Lew," Norman said without further prelude.

Mary was grateful that he willingly plunged in, since Henry had expressed concern on their way over from the restaurant that they really should leave the island soon.

"Lew Nelson was our great-uncle," she said. "His older brother Charles was our grandfather."

Norman returned Mary's gaze, and she noted a steeliness in his green eyes. His shaggy mane of white hair gave him a fierce look, but she'd noticed a bit of red lingering in the locks on the back of his head.

"Never had much use for Lew, to be honest. The way he treated Ruth—your aunt Maude—was shameful."

"We never saw that side of him." Mary kept her voice even and hoped his allegations wouldn't upset her sister. "Could you tell us more, Mr. Liddell? You see, our folks never mentioned any of this. In fact, we thought Aunt Maude died in 1950, and whenever we visited Uncle Lew, he seemed like a perfectly reasonable man."

"I suppose he changed. I can even hope he learned a lesson when she left him." Norman let out a big sigh and leaned back in his chair. "He criticized her constantly. Wore her down to where she thought she was worthless."

"But her art," Betty said. "We have some of her paintings from that period, and they're wonderful!"

"So they were." Norman's eyes drifted to a painting hanging over the brick fireplace, and Mary followed his gaze.

"That's hers, isn't it?" she asked.

"Yes, from a happier time."

Mary stood and walked closer to take in the bright, sunny oil painting. It showed the Nantucket harbor with the Brant Point lighthouse in the background and a fishing boat coming in to its mooring. On the shore stood a blonde woman. She wasn't wearing the blue-and-yellow sundress—she had on a billowing white top and blue capris—and her face was turned away from the viewer, but Mary knew her at once.

"That's Maude," Betty said.

Mary nodded.

"And that's my boat," Norman added from his chair. "She was waiting for me when I came in every night. She painted it the summer after we came here. Those were happy days."

"Can you tell us about it?" Mary asked.

"Not much to tell. We fell in love, but we kept it secret. I guess we both felt guilty. She didn't even tell her best friend. I moved out here with my cousin to put some distance between us, but I couldn't stay away from her. Every time I went back to Ivy Bay to see my folks, I saw her, and pretty soon I was making excuses to go more often. We loved each other, but... " He looked up and blinked behind his glasses. "When I got to my parents' house that night, she called me early. I hadn't expected to see her until the next day, when Lew left for work, but she said to come over then. She said Lew had hit her and left in a huff. She didn't expect he'd be back for hours, and she was packing her things. She wanted me to get her out of there. I was furious, I'll tell you. I wanted to confront him, but she was wiser than me. After she talked me down, I could see she was right—it would be better to just get her away, without giving him any clues as to whom she went with or where."

"You did a good job," Mary said. "It took us more than sixty years to figure it out."

"We heard that Lew spread it around that she was dead," Norman said.

"That's right. We have the guest book from the funeral."

"It's kind of funny," Norman said. "Ruth wanted to tell people it wasn't true, but we both decided not to. Until my cousin found out the police were looking at Lew to see if he'd done something to her."

"That's when Maude sent the letter to the Provincetown police, with the picture of her holding a newspaper."

"Yes. She didn't mind him suffering a little, but she sure didn't want him charged with murder when she was perfectly healthy and happy."

"The detective told me about it," Mary said.

"We had a friend who was going into Boston, and we asked her to mail it from there, so it wouldn't be postmarked Nantucket."

"I think that letter went a long way to subduing Uncle Lew," Mary said. "I never knew him to be violent, although some of his neighbors did tell us he'd had a short temper."

"Yes, well, hitting a woman who was in the family way—I don't care how mad he was. There's no excuse for that."

"So, she *was* expecting when she left him?" Mary nodded. "She put herself into two of the paintings we have, and in one she does look pregnant. We wondered about that. To our knowledge, she hadn't had any children with Uncle Lew."

"Well, this one's all mine," Norman said. "You only have to look at the hair to know it's true."

"Dad," Brad said, frowning.

Mary gulped at the old man's frankness. She couldn't think of a single thing to say.

Norman smiled. "I just wish I could have seen Lew's face when those cops came sniffing around. I'll bet he scrambled some, trying to convince them she was alive—after he'd pretended to bury her. We should have let him suffer longer, but Ruth said the further it went, the more attention it would draw to her when she told them she was alive. So we told the cops."

Mary resumed her seat on the sofa with Henry, but Betty had moved to the adjacent wall and was studying another painting. This one showed a marsh bird on its nest, and the style was quite different from Maude's, soft-toned but realistic.

"Tara Liddell," Betty said. "That's the signature. Was this done by a family member?"

Deena, Bradley's wife, rose and went to stand beside her. "She's our granddaughter. She shows great promise, don't you think?"

"It's beautiful. The detail is remarkable." Betty lingered for a moment, then went back to her chair.

"She's going to art school in Boston," Brad said. "It's expensive though. We wish we could help, but...well, the fishing business isn't as profitable as it used to be."

"She's your son's daughter?" Mary asked, figuring the relationship because the young woman carried the Liddell name.

"That's right," Deena said, smiling broadly. "She's our pride and joy—she and her brother. He's not artistic though. Wants to carry on the fishing business, if it's still there when he's ready."

Again, Mary wished they had more time to learn about the Liddell family. She glanced at Henry, and he smiled placidly, as though they had all the time in the world, but she knew he was thinking about the lowering sun and the winds on the Sound.

"Would you mind if I took a few photos?" She reached into her bag for her camera.

"I guess that'd be all right," Brad said. "What do you think, Dad?"

"I suppose so, though you understand we're no relation."

"I know, but I've looked for you so long, and I'm so happy to meet you. I'd love to have a photo of you to put with Aunt Maude's letters and the other mementos we've collected."

She photographed Norman, his son, and Deena, and also several of Maude's paintings that hung in various spots in their house.

"This one's my favorite," Norman said, indicating one that hung in his bedroom, where he could see it when he awoke each morning. "It's a self-portrait of her, holding Brad."

Mary gazed at the sweet mother-and-child painting and smiled. That would have been a nice addition to Linda Freeman's album.

"You know, some of her paintings sold for four and five thousand dollars," Norman said with pride. "That gallery up in Maine couldn't get enough from her."

"But we kept a few," Deena said.

Brad laughed. "Mom always said they were my inheritance, and if things got too tough, I could sell them."

"What a wonderful gift," Betty said.

"Well, that day may be here pretty soon," Deena said a bit glumly.

Mary told them about the RML painting of Nantucket she had bought from the gallery in Barnstable. "Do you know how many paintings she sold in her lifetime?"

"I'm not sure," Norman said. "I know she sent at least a hundred to Maine. Her old friend from the gallery in Ivy Bay moved up there and wanted to sell her work."

"Yes, I know about that," Mary said. "She must have kept in contact with him after she moved out here."

"For a while, but then he moved away from Ivy Bay, and she had me looking for a new place to sell her work. She didn't want to put it in Ivy Bay anymore, because too many people there knew her. Or Provincetown, of course—Lew would have seen it, for sure. She didn't dare to sell them anywhere on the Cape. And then Ludwig saw one of her new paintings, after he'd moved to Maine. Ruth had sent it to someone up there in Boothbay Harbor. Well, he knew right away it was hers, and he bribed the gallery owner to give him her address. He wrote and said he'd opened a new gallery in Camden and wanted to carry her paintings. He begged her to send him some, and after a while, she did. He was always her best customer. She kept track of her shipments, but I don't think she ever counted up the total."

"And she must have done quite a few when she lived in Ivy Bay and Provincetown," Mary said.

"I guess so. I have no idea, really, but you're right. She did quite a few before we were married. Before she came out here with me, that is." Norman smiled ruefully. "It was almost ten years before we could get married."

"Now, that's one thing we hadn't verified," Betty said.

"Tell us about it, won't you?" Mary asked.

Norman shrugged. "After a few years, Ruth said she was tired of pretending and wanted to make it legal. She had a lawyer contact Lew, and he agreed to a divorce, that's all. We were sort of surprised he gave in so easily, but I guess by then he'd accepted things. We were married in 1959, here on the island."

"Now that I know when and where, it shouldn't be hard to find the records," Mary said. She caught Henry stealing a glance at his watch. "I hate to cut this short, but I'm afraid we have to get going if we want to reach the mainland before nightfall."

"Oh, sure," Norman said. "Time and tide, and all that."

"It was nice meeting you folks and to learn more about Ruth," Deena said, reaching for their coats.

"I'm real sorry about the way I greeted you," Brad said.

"That's all right," Mary told him. "And we really would like to have you visit us in Ivy Bay. If you want to see the paintings we have, or just visit, come next time you're on the Cape."

"We'd love to meet your granddaughter too," Betty added.

Mary smiled. "Perhaps we could drive to Boston one day and take her off campus for lunch."

"She'd sure like that," Deena said.

"Do you remember Maude's friend—that is, Ruth's friend, Elle Wetherly?" Betty asked Norman.

"Sure. Ruth was afraid after we left that Elle would figure out where she was and tell Lew. But I guess she never did."

"No, she didn't," Betty said. "She still cares about your wife and wonders what happened."

"Ruth actually wrote to her once, to tell her we were married. That was ten years after she left, of course, and things had settled down with Lew. But her letter came back, with no forwarding address."

"That must have been after Elle moved to Connecticut," Betty said.

"What a shame they lost contact that way," Mary said.

Norman nodded. "There weren't any home computers then, and communication between the island and the mainland wasn't always reliable. Ruth didn't want people to know she was asking around either. Even though Lew had cooperated, she still didn't want him to know where she was living."

"Well, it will mean a lot to Elle to know that Maude was happy," Mary assured him.

"I'm sure she only wanted the best for her friend," Norman said.

"Yes, and she never told Lew anything as far as your romance was concerned. Do you mind if I send her a picture of you and Brad?"

"Sure, go ahead," Norman said.

While Mary snapped a few more photos, Deena called a taxi for them to hasten their way to the boat landing. They took their leave of the Liddells, and Henry soon had the *Misty Horizon* under way. The temperature had fallen about twenty degrees, and the three of them stayed in the pilothouse and the cabin, drinking hot tea from the thermos bottle. They also enjoyed the remains of the picnic lunch they hadn't eaten, having opted for a full meal at a restaurant instead.

"I've been thinking about the house," Mary said.

"Uncle Lew's house?" Betty's eyebrows arched. "That's funny. So have I."

"The Liddells didn't spell it out, but it seems to me they're having a hard time financially."

Betty nodded. "Are you thinking what I'm thinking?"

"If it's to give them the house, I am." Mary smiled. "Otherwise, I have no clue."

"That was it. They could either go and live there or sell it and use the money to help them stay on Nantucket."

"And maybe help out a little with Tara's art school tuition," Mary added.

"I'd like that." Betty nodded firmly. "Let's do it."

The breakwater and lighthouse were soon behind them. On Nantucket Sound, the seas were fairly calm, and Henry pushed the throttle as hard as he dared. Even so, darkness had fallen by the time they tied up in Hyannis.

Mary drove home, feeling sleepy but content with their day's work. When they pulled into the driveway next to Henry's car, she turned to look at him.

"It's late, Henry. Why don't you stay and have a bite with us?"

"Oh, I'd better get on home, but thanks just the same."

"Thank you so much for taking us," Betty said. "I enjoyed the boat ride tremendously."

"Anytime, ladies."

Henry got out and took the picnic basket inside for them. He placed it on the kitchen table and smiled at Mary. "I was planning to fish tomorrow, but Brad Liddell said it's going to snow, and I don't like the look of the sky."

"Not many stars tonight," she agreed.

"If it's even hinting of snow, I'll probably stay home. And you never know, I might come around the bookshop."

"It's a nice place to be on a cold, windy day." She watched him walk out to his car, waved, and closed the door.

"Well," Betty said. "We finally know what happened."

"Yes. Not the ideal ending to the story, but better than I expected, to be truthful."

Betty nodded. "What would you think of hanging that painting you bought in the living room? Between the windows on the east wall, maybe?"

Mary turned with a smile. "I think that would be a fantastic spot for it. All our friends could enjoy Aunt Maude's view of Nantucket."

ABOUT THE AUTHOR

Susan Page Davis is the author of more than forty novels in the romance, mystery, suspense, and historical romance genres. A Maine native, she now lives in western Kentucky. The move has taken some getting used to. She swapped hurricanes for tornado warnings, and mosquitoes for poisonous snakes. Overall, she enjoys the milder winters and being closer to her grandchildren. Susan is a past winner of the Carol Award, the Will Rogers Medallion for Western Fiction, and the Inspirational Readers' Choice Award. Visit her Web site at susanpagedavis.com.

A CONVERSATION WITH SUSAN PAGE DAVIS

———— ◆◆ ————

Q: *What's your favorite vacation spot?*

A: I love traveling and seeing new things. One of the nicest places I've discovered so far was Prince Edward Island, where I spent a week with two of my children. It's beautiful!

Q: *What was something interesting or important that you learned while researching and writing this novel?*

A: My brother, who is a retired coast guard officer and spent some time stationed in the Cape Cod area, gave me a crash course on navigation in New England. I'm just glad that in the book, Henry is driving the boat, not me!

Q: *If you could go to Ivy Bay, which place/shop would you visit first?*

A: After Mary's bookshop, of course, I'd love to stop by the gallery and browse the Cape Cod art.

Q: *Mary often goes to the library when sleuthing out a mystery. What's the library like in your hometown?*

A: I have to go to the next larger town to find a public library, but it's a nice one. I enjoy browsing there and looking up points of local history. The staff is very considerate of local authors, too, and holds events where the patrons can meet and talk to them.

Q: *What's your favorite type of book to read?*
A: I read lots of different sorts of books, but mysteries are high on my list.

Q: *Mary loves to snuggle up with a cup of tea or a quilt and read at the end of the day. How do you like to spend the quiet hours of an evening at home?*
A: I'm with Mary. That sounds just about perfect to me.

SUNDAY PUDDING

❖◆❖

This was a favorite recipe of my mother's when I was a child.

On Saturday night, combine one-half pound of marshmallows, quartered (or two cups mini marshmallows) with one pint frozen or fresh strawberries (slightly mashed and slightly sweetened). Let stand overnight.

On Sunday morning, add one-half pint of slightly sweetened whipped cream. Fold into fruit and marshmallow mixture. Chill. (Do not substitute nondairy whipped topping for the real whipped cream. It will curdle.)

Variations: Add crushed pineapple, maraschino cherries, and chopped nuts, or add crushed pineapple and sliced bananas.

FROM THE GUIDEPOSTS ARCHIVE

◆◆◆

The young man saith unto him, All these things have I kept from my youth up: what lack I yet? —Matthew 19:20 (KJV)

Our move was almost complete, except for the attic. All four members of the family had sorted through their personal things, so I didn't expect to find much up there. On this final day my father had come up from New York City to help us finish the move.

My body was tired and sore and my spirit yearned for some summer fun, but I kept thinking, *This is it. This is the last hurrah of moving.* I walked up to the attic with my dad; the heat made it almost unbearable. We were dismayed to find that it was filled with boxes of all kinds and sizes, all of them empty.

"You have more boxes here than a store," my father said. Dad had worked for thirty-five years in the fabric retail business; he knew about boxes. "How did you end up with so many?"

We'd been saving them since we arrived in Carmel, New York, seven years ago—for the big move. And here we'd almost finished it without remembering they were there. Dad walked around, picking up boxes and repeating his question. I started laughing. It became the joke of the day.

The experience got me thinking about some of the things in my life that hold me back. It's been a long time since I've taken inventory of the things that are stored in my heart. What have I been holding on to that is no longer of any value or benefit? What do I need to remove, so I can grow in my faith?

Lord, help me to examine my heart and to let go of things that take up space that could be filled with Your love and grace.

—Pablo Diaz

A NOTE FROM THE EDITORS

We hope you enjoy Secrets of Mary's Bookshop, created by the Books and Inspirational Media Division of Guideposts, a nonprofit organization. In all of our books, magazines and outreach efforts, we aim to deliver inspiration and encouragement, help you grow in your faith, and celebrate God's love in every aspect of your daily life.

Thank you for making a difference with your purchase of this book, which helps fund our many outreach programs to the military, prisons, hospitals, nursing homes and schools. To learn more, visit GuidepostsFoundation.org.

We also maintain many useful and uplifting online resources. Visit Guideposts.org to read true stories of hope and inspiration, access OurPrayer network, sign up for free newsletters, download free e-books, join our Facebook community, and follow our stimulating blogs.

To learn about other Guideposts publications, including the best-selling devotional *Daily Guideposts*, go to ShopGuideposts.org, call (800) 932-2145 or write to Guideposts, PO Box 5815, Harlan, Iowa 51593.